steaming ahead

Cora Sandel was born in Norway in 1880 and died in Sweden in 1974. She is the author of the following collections of short stories: *En blå soffa* (*A Blue Sofa*), 1927; *Carmen och Maja* (*Carmen and Maja*), 1932; *Tack dodtorn* (*Thank you, Doctor*), 1935; *Djur som jag känt* (*Animals I have known*), 1945; *Figurer på mörk botten* (*Figures Against a Dark Background*), 1949; *Vårt krångliga liv* (*Our Complicated Life*), 1963, and also of the following full-length works which have been translated into English: *Köp inte Dondi* (*The Leech*), 1958 and the novels in the Alberta trilogy, published simultaneously by The Women's Press in 1980: *Alberta and Jacob, Alberta and Freedom* and *Alberta Alone.*

Cora Sandel
Krane's Café
An Interior With Figures

Translated from the Norwegian by
Elizabeth Rokkan

The Women's Press

Published in Great Britain by
The Women's Press Limited 1984
A member of the Namara Group
124 Shoreditch High Street, London E1 6JE

First published in English by Peter Owen Limited, London 1968
Original title *Kranes Konditori*

British Library Cataloguing in Publication Data

Sandel, Cora
    Krane's Café.
    I. Title
    839.8′2372 [F]   PT8959.F2

    ISBN 0-7043-3940-4

    Printed in Great Britain
    by Nene Litho and bound by
    Woolnough Bookbinding, both of
    Wellingborough, Northants

If people can see that you're suffering, you're finished.

Agnes Mowinckel

Poverty is terrible. Of all so-called misfortunes, it's the one that affects you most deeply internally.

Hjalmar Söderberg

SCENE ONE

There's a lot to be heard before your ears drop off.

A true saying, as they all discovered at Krane's café during those two days. They were quite exhausted afterwards.

That's where it happened.

Not everything, of course, but more than enough. Talk about washing dirty linen. We thought we knew about most things in a small town like this. What we didn't know, we could work out. It's a bit much to have it all confirmed and more added, and the whole thing turned inside out and upside down, all at once.

Nobody knows for certain what went on at Rivermouth besides all this. Only that something did. Something must have.

Mrs Berg Junior, that little goose, goes round hinting that with a little goodwill from various quarters the matter would never have gone so far. If you ask her what she means, she has no suggestions to offer. 'I don't really know,' she says. 'I just think everyone was so unkind to Mrs Stordal.'

'How, unkind?'

'I don't know, but . . .'

Mrs Berg Junior is a fool. Quite pretty to look at, but insignificant. Young Berg married her for her money, everyone knows that. No need to bother your head about what she thinks.

Anyway, was there no goodwill? Or patience or forbear-

7

ance, and I don't know what else besides? What about Mrs Breien? And Solicitor Buck? Can people go any further than they did? Buck was tough to start with, but was that to be wondered at?

Torsen? Yes, of course, there was Torsen too. Torsen was touching. An unusually good soul, Torsen, let me tell you.

If anyone's to be blamed it has to be Mrs Krane. If she had had the sense to exert a little authority at the right moment, much could have been avoided. But she *cried*, poor thing, cried almost the whole time. They say she came up with some nonsense about a voice – that dreadful fellow's voice, if you please – that had affected her so strangely. The sort of thing she'd do better to keep quiet about. She was frightened too, she said. But good heavens, we have the police in town, after all, and doctors in case of emergency. In the end she was frightened of herself, she said. Have you ever heard such foolishness?

But she's reached that certain age, you know. Probably didn't quite know what she was doing. Many of them get like that. They're the ones who lose their wits.

She was clever to get rid of the crowd from Rivermouth; fair's fair. But you can't put the clock back. The situation was past saving by that time. You do more harm than good by being too kind, and that's for sure.

Krane was in Southfjord. You can't blame him. So unfortunate that he should have been away. He's no heavyweight, but he knows how to be firm, and a man's a man, there's no getting away from that.

He was angry when he came home and heard the whole story. Goodness gracious, say the people who live on the other side of the wall, that nice man! He has to consider his business since the alterations, that's what it is. Clever man in his way. He was quite justified, you must admit.

After all, it wasn't just the scandal itself. It was all the uncertainty about whether everything would turn out all

8

right. Scarcely a week to the Centenary Ball, the biggest ball in the history of the town. In other circumstances an example ought to have been made of somebody. No one ought to have set foot inside Krane's café or Mrs Stordal's house again. But what can you do? The top dressmaker in the place, the only café where one can possibly go? Obviously that sort of thing mustn't happen too often.

Every crumb wasn't actually heard or seen, of course. But even those who have difficulty adding up can make two and two equal four. And there were three of them there, Mrs Krane herself, Miss Larsen and Miss Sønstegård. Or Larsen and Sønstegård as the regulars say. The one caught a hint here, the other there. And if you set your mind on keeping your eyes and ears open . . .

Several of the people who came and went were able to make their contribution afterwards as well. Mrs Breien first and foremost. And the Bucks.

Stordal wasn't one to keep his mouth shut either. Why should he? If anyone was treated unjustly, surely it was that man, and on all sides. Just take Elise Oyen. Such behaviour!

Now she and Lydersen gossip right and left, determined to get their oar in as well. But surely no one pays much attention to what those two say. They have their own affairs to claw over like cats. Yes indeed, quite disgraceful!

Makes you wonder whether they ought to be reported to the police. If only it weren't so unpleasant.

But in any case, you needn't be any the wiser for hearing anything. On many points you're just as much in the dark as you were before, so much was new and unexpected. Nobody can remember everything either, you may remember it wrong and use your imagination a little. In fact you're left with the bits of a puzzle, and you don't quite know how to put them together.

But everyone hasn't talked it over with everyone else yet. That fellow Gjør? Oh, him! Odd that he should suddenly have put in an appearance and interfered as he did. But we were given the explanation for *that*. Gracious heavens!

Extraordinary that people can forget themselves like that. But they were under provocation, and much was at stake. Not only for the individual, for the whole town.

And that's no exaggeration.

There can't be many people who are not familiar with Krane's café. Since the alterations everyone goes there, high and low. And that's as it should be, so long as they behave themselves.

So far, Krane and Mrs Krane have done their best to keep standards at a respectable level. It can be a bit uproarious in the evenings occasionally, but people always exaggerate. The Stordal affair, on the other hand, is one of those embarrassing events that unfortunately cannot be called into question. If Mrs Krane shows the same lack of judgment a second time, we all ought to agree on one course of action : get up, go, and never come back.

You say you can't always tell who's sitting in the parlour when the door's shut?

Oh yes, you'll be able to tell. If not from anything else, you'll see it from the way Larsen and Sønstegård behave. They've said they're not going to serve just anybody any more : they'll go on strike. And where will Krane find anyone else who's efficient and not a union member? He understands the situation, he'll keep order.

And that door shouldn't be closed all the time. Somebody ought to keep their eye on a door like that.

In case there's anyone who hasn't heard, or who perhaps is quite unfamiliar with Krane's, we should first of all begin with the shop. They've made it attractive and spacious, with small tables dotted all over the room like the cafés down south. Lighter too, since Bleken, the master-builder, suggested knocking out two large windows in the wall facing the quay. Before that you could only look out on the High Street, and it was quite dark at the back of the premises. Now the sun streams in, you have a view of the mountains on the other side of the fjord, and on the days when the coastal steamer comes in you can watch it arriving and all the passengers going ashore. Not to mention the cruise ships in summer and the other boats that come in – the local steamers, the Hamburg line. Splendid idea of Bleken's.

Between the windows stands the big radiogram, which is danced to in the evenings and gets foreign stations. Above that the mirror, the largest in town besides Mrs Stordal's. But after all, she's a dressmaker.

Against the inner wall the new counter with cakes, sandwiches under glass and the till, the shelves with boxes of chocolate tastefully displayed at an angle, and the wall clock. Farther on the sliding door, the one you only have to push once and it's open.

It's probably that push which people find tempting. The door is a novelty. You have to go to the most modern villas to find one like it. It has its drawbacks, it lets too much through, sounds in particular, but that was almost an advantage on this occasion. Besides, the heavy old portiere still hangs behind it and can be pulled across when necessary.

And when it's not necessary? It won't happen again, you may be quite certain.

In what used to be 'the back room' everything is as it used to be. Only the name has been changed. Now it's called 'the parlour'. The wallpaper is the brown one, patterned with large flowers, that everyone remembers from his childhood. The console table with the mirror above it, that Krane's father once bought at an auction of Consul Klykken's belongings, stands as usual in one corner. The faded reproductions of the Lake of Geneva and the Gulf of Naples hang as they have always hung, slightly crooked. The two marble tables at which we used to eat cream slices in our schooldays are still the same. The one nearest the window is cracked right across to this day.

It's all a bit heavy and dark, but there's a certain tradition about it. Krane and Bleken are said to have plans for altering that part gradually too, to make it light and functional, but there are plenty of people who advise them against it. A private party, for instance, is pleasant enough in the parlour as it is now. Functional? There'd be no portière then, I suppose? Or perhaps they'd have those thin, light things that flutter in the slightest draught? No, with all respect for modernity, the old has its charm too. And we count on people who know how to behave.

But in the corner of the shop on the side towards the quay Bleken has put in a big glass revolving door, like the ones they have in hotels and banks down south. It's this, more than anything, that gives the café its stylish appearance. Another of those ideas of his that will gradually come to modernize the whole town. Stordal, with his passion for those old Empire doors down in Fjord Street, would never have hit on anything like that. If he had been in charge of the alterations it would probably have been turned into a museum of ancient architectural styles.

They've installed central heating – a tremendous improvement. They don't have that, even at the Grand. Krane knows how things should be done. People say he's making a fortune. A bit of an exaggeration perhaps, but anyone can see that business is good, especially since he started to do cooked lunches and introduced dancing in the evenings. He's always been known for his cakes, like his father before him. He's had a wine licence for a long time. This might have led to unpleasantness formerly, on Saturdays and national holidays. Now nearly everyone behaves properly, even though they say the youngsters are a little rowdy late at night.

If only the Stordal affair had never happened . . .

They were sitting there one Saturday morning during the quiet period after lunch : Mrs Krane behind the till, knitting a pullover as always when she has a moment to spare, Larsen and Sønstegård folding paper napkins. You can never have too many of those. It was early spring and the sun was shining. There were birch leaves and pussy willow on the tables. You could feel that summer was not far away.

Not a customer in the place except for Mrs Katinka Stordal. Or Mrs Katinka, as many people say. She had been sitting so long over an empty plate and an empty wine glass in the parlour, that Larsen had found herself an errand and casually peeped in through the half-open sliding door. Mrs Katinka was sitting with her head in her hands and did not look up. Larsen shrugged her shoulders at Mrs Krane in despair. Mrs Krane looked up at the clock and sighed.

That had been some time ago. Mrs Krane, who is at a fidgety age, glanced at the clock again and could not help clicking her tongue, as she usually does when something goes too far : 'Tut, tut, tut, oh dear, oh dear.'

'She's been sitting there for at least half an hour now,' whispered Larsen as she folded. 'And when she has so much to do, and Torsen helping her as well.'

Sønstegård sucked at her tooth – she has a habit of sucking at it, but that's a detail after all – and muttered, 'Probably got a thirst and nothing in the house. People will come and take their dress lengths away, just as they did the last time. Nice thing to happen, now of all times.'

'Fancy her being so good at dressmaking,' whispered Larsen. 'A genius at dressmaking.'

'Can be when she wants to, of course. Plenty of people like that. But a man looks for more than proficiency.' Sønstegård sucked at her tooth thoughtfully.

'I understand that. I realize that. A man wants a bit of comfort, that's what he wants.'

'Comfort, did you say?' Sønstegård almost forgot to whisper. 'It's no wonder that man left home. Nothing but a sloven. Doesn't even go to bed like other folk. Stays up all night, that's what she does.'

Larsen completely forgot to whisper. She exclaimed, 'Oh, it can't be easy to be a man sometimes.'

'Shush, are you crazy? She might hear you!' whispered Mrs Krane and Sønstegård in unison. Larsen always had to be so sympathetic. It was a rather dangerous side to her character. She was fairly new to the town too, and the kind who tries to look younger than she is. Now she was holding her hand in front of her mouth in a horrified gesture.

'I didn't mean *that* exactly,' said Sønstegård coldly. 'She won't put up with anything *risqué*.'

'I didn't mean *that* either,' whispered Larsen back, a little piqued at being corrected. 'But that's just why it must be difficult for a man. If only the late mornings, and nothing tidy.'

Sønstegård sucked at her tooth without replying. Larsen was not going to wriggle out of it so easily.

Mrs Krane looked at the clock again, shook her head, put down her pullover and tapped on the wall with her knitting needle. 'It's almost half past one, Mrs Stordal.'

'Thank you, I know.'

'Tut, tut, tut.' Mrs Krane went over to the door, her voice sharp with nervousness. 'I was only afraid you'd forgotten the time. Just thought I'd let you know. Thought I heard someone say they were going to you for a fitting at one o'clock. Wasn't it Mrs Buck?'

'I'm going, I'm going,' said Mrs Stordal. She looked up listlessly for a moment, and stayed where she was. It was one of those days when she looks much older than she really is. After all, she's not much more than forty-odd and often manages to look quite young. Today she was old. She had obviously thrown on her clothes in a hurry. An odd person. At times almost well-dressed; not chic perhaps, but correct. At other times . . .

She made no move to go. On the contrary, she mechanically inspected her glass, which was quite empty, looked in her handbag – but presumably found nothing, for she put it down with a sigh – and settled down once more, hunched up over the table.

'Like water off a duck's back,' muttered Mrs Krane, resignedly resuming her place behind the till with her pullover.

Then Larsen had to be sympathetic again. She remarked quite loudly, 'Wasn't Mrs Buck talking about it to Mrs Breien, then, that her dress had been promised in good time?'

In her eagerness she raised her voice even higher. 'Yes, it's a busy time. Centenary Ball and everything. Spring too. But it's nice for people to have work. There's plenty without it.'

The last sentence was terribly loud.

'Now then!' said Sønstegård quietly and sharply. She could not stand little Larsen's continual meddling. It wasn't suitable either; Mrs Krane had taken charge of the matter herself.

'We must do what we can,' said Larsen in injured tones. 'Beginning to be terribly quiet in here,' she said after a while, to show she had not taken offence.

'You *are* getting demanding. Isn't it nice to have a bit of peace?'

'Peace? Time enough for peace when you're old. And demanding? Yes, I *am* demanding.' Larsen hummed, then announced, 'So are you, don't try to tell me anything different.'

'I *am* old, you see. That's when you're through with all that tomfoolery. They can't get round me any more.'

'Who can't?'

'Yes, who?'

Larsen coughed at this point.

'It never pays to be demanding.'

'I'm not so sure about that.'

'You'll soon find out.'

'Oh, what a bore you are with all this bitterness!' exclaimed Larsen. Then she sighed. 'Soon it'll be summer, and people will be moving up to their cottages. Out on picnics day and night. And here we shall sit with Mrs Katinka the only customer. But *I* shan't be bitter, no indeed.'

'Then we shall have all the gentlemen here at noon every blessed day. The whole lot. They don't go all the way back to their cottages for lunch. And what about the tourists? And our old customers from before the alterations? They'll come when it's not so fearfully genteel here any more. And I like *them*, I must say.'

'Don't you think I like them too?'

'There's that fellow Stordal.'

Larsen craned her neck. 'Is he coming here?'

'God knows. No, he's going the other way.'

'To meet the children perhaps. It's a long time since he brought either of them here.'

'Probably thinks it's embarrassing.'

'Does he owe very much, do you think?'

'God knows. He's signed chits so many times. Krane did send him a bill once.' Sønstegård sucked at her tooth and shook her head. 'I'm sorry for that fellow Stordal.'

'Yes, poor fellow.'

Larsen and Sønstegård could sit gossiping, thanks to Mrs Krane, who was completely taken up with listening to see whether Mrs Katinka was going or not; thanks too to the fact that they made up their own little trade union. There was a rule about not discussing the customers. It's not correct for a restaurant, Krane had said.

As if neither of *them* gossiped now and again.

'They say the wives are so annoyed when the men don't come home for lunch,' said Larsen.

'The wives had better watch their tongues. Think of the money *they* spend here on coffee and cakes, mornings and afternoons.'

'So they do !' exclaimed Larsen, struck by the thought.

It was then that the man they call Bowler Hat came into the café. And it isn't easy to show the door to people like that, who don't know any better themselves, however much you may feel like it. Not until they've behaved badly, at any rate.

He elbowed his way through the revolving door, in his usual manner, went across to the counter, and stood there inspecting the sandwiches. Larsen and Sønstegård became slightly agitated, nudging each other and shaking their heads. Neither of them wanted to serve him.

He's not what you'd call polite. He stood there with his hat on and his hands in his trouser pockets, chewing on a cigarette. Tall and thin, in worn clothes, his collar turned up and no overcoat : not a customer any respectable place would be proud of. Not old, but with an emaciated face, worn down by life. Probably been through all sorts of experiences. If only he behaved himself properly . . .

He pointed at a sandwich and said, in his Swedish accent, 'That one, please, with egg and anchovy, give me that one.' Then he went straight across to the radiogram and fiddled with the knobs. He went over to feel the radiator too, which really was none of his business. Mrs Krane signed to the others with her knitting needle that they must be kind and take no notice.

The man elbowed his way through the half-open sliding door into the parlour and sat down at the window table, slouching, his hat still on his head and his legs sprawled in front of him. Mrs Krane leaned forward, took it all in and said, 'Tut, tut, tut'. From the very beginning she had a feeling that something dreadful was going to happen, she said afterwards. So how she could have let matters go as far as they did is beyond understanding.

He sat as if his hand was padlocked inside his trouser pocket. If it hadn't been for the plate and the sandwich, both of them would probably have remained buried in his trousers. What a way to sit! He glanced across at Katinka a couple of times, but she was looking elsewhere and seemed almost embarrassed. Mrs Krane thought that even though she hadn't left before, she'd be bound to do so *now*. This was one of the things Mrs Krane insisted on later in her defence, and at that moment there might have been something in it. He merely chewed his cigarette.

Out in the shop Larsen said, 'That ill-mannered fellow. Here he is again. And we have to serve people like that. Can't he go to Hansen's? That's the place for his kind. Their cakes aren't too bad. They haven't a revolving door, it's true—'

'Nor a radiator, nor a wine licence,' said Sønstegård.

In the distance Mrs Krane was gesticulating helplessly with her knitting needle. 'Mr Krane doesn't want any commotion, you know how Mr Krane is,' she whispered penetratingly.

But it was really she herself who wanted no commotion.

Inside the parlour the man banged on his plate with his fork. Mrs Krane gesticulated imploringly.

'It's not my table,' said Larsen firmly, sure of her rights, and Sønstegård set off with reluctance.

'One coffee, two cream puffs,' prescribed Bowler Hat, sitting there in that improper manner of his, with his legs sprawling and his hat on his head. If only Mrs Krane would say something about that hat, at least. Foolish of her.

'We only have cream puffs at Christmas time.' Sønstegård had no intention of understanding more than was strictly necessary. He might as well be discouraged from coming.

'If it's biscuits you want, we have them,' she informed

him curtly, without looking at him. Her orders were to be obliging to the customers, and you get into the habit of that.

But Bowler Hat was truculent. He mimicked her : 'Biscuits? Damn it all, I want big cakes, proper cakes, with whipped cream on top. Lots of whipped cream. *Två*. Two. *Genast*. At once, I mean. Understand?'

At last he took off his hat, putting it on the table. Despairingly Sønstegård looked across at Katinka. She wasn't the sort who ought to be encouraged either, but now . . .

Katinka did not return her glance. Sønstegård departed in high dudgeon, opening the door wide as she passed. An uninterrupted view was needed. The door slid into the wall with a tremendous clatter.

Katinka was about to leave. At least that's what it looked like when Sønstegård went, for she had collected her gloves and handbag and buttoned up her jacket. At the same time she seemed as if she hadn't the energy to move, as if something were weighing her down.

Out in the shop the loudspeaker was blaring forth earsplittingly '— large ox-hides, forty-five *øre* the kilo. Cowhides, raw, fifty *øre*. Calfskins, raw, two *kroner* seventy-five the piece. Horse-hides, top quality, ten *kroner*. Pigs, stock, meat only . . .'

For Bowler Hat had been over to the radio. He was obviously not very practised in finding the right wavelength.

'Whatever next!' exclaimed Larsen.

'Without heads and trotters, hide and chitterlings included in the price . . .'

'No one can stand this,' announced Larsen with decision. And although it was not really done to reprimand a customer, she ran across and turned the knob.

'That's all right, *I* can stand anything,' Bowler Hat informed her from inside the parlour.

'But *we* can't, you see.'

Larsen was not so practised either, so far as the new

instrument was concerned. 'Goat's cheese, one *krone* precisely,' screamed the loudspeaker even more penetratingly than before.

'Stop that racket!' Larsen twiddled angrily and impatiently, conjuring up a variety of noises, and finally found 'Chant Hindou' – for violin – by Rimsky-Korsakov.

'Oh, what a relief! It's Copenhagen. If we're to listen to anything, it had better be music at any rate.'

'There we are, that's how it ought to sound. Other people never understand those thingummyjigs,' said Bowler Hat to Sønstegård, who had come back with his order. 'Soon makes the girls lovesick, doesn't it, that sort of stuff?'

Who replies to that sort of utterance? Not Sønstegård, anyway. 'I think it's getting late, Mrs Stordal,' she said to Katinka.

And would you believe it, Mrs Stordal put her money on the table without a word.

'Thank you.' Sønstegård picked up her plate and glass and went. In the shop she handed the money over to Mrs Krane, who triumphantly jingled the till. Now they would soon be rid of Mrs Katinka, surely?

It was then Bowler Hat got to his feet and shouted, 'Baboon!'

Sønstegård had to conclude that this was addressed to her. But she had no time to collect her wits before the door clattered to again with a bang and the portière was drawn behind it. They could hear it clearly, because the rings move sluggishly along the rod.

It will surprise no one that they were vexed; nor that all three of them put their ears to the door. You can't allow anything whatsoever to happen, absolutely uncontrolled in there.

'Turn off the radio, please,' said Mrs Krane nervously. Larsen went over and did so. It had started playing heaven knows what, to no purpose.

Katinka and Bowler Hat must have been near the door,

both of them, for they heard clearly when, in a voice quite different from his normal one – a soft, polite, and incredible though it may seem, almost pleasant tone – he asked, 'May I offer you a pastry? And a cup of coffee? Come now, will you allow me?'

And Katinka must have been a little drunk, even though she had had only one glass, no more. Otherwise she would have left without a word in reply. She's not the kind to pick up men, at any rate not in recent years. The song the boys sing after her sometimes in the street is nonsense : fair's fair, it's the remnants of old, forgotten gossip, mixed up with the fact that she drinks. Now the ladies heard her say, a little uncertainly, a little hesitatingly, 'It's very kind of you, but I've just—'

'Do you have to go, just because someone else comes in? Isn't it done to talk to other people?'

'I was just *about* to go.'

'Yes, indeed you were, and when I came you hurried up. I know all about that. In other countries, in the south, it's not like that. There people talk to each other. Here in Scandinavia you're treated like the plague if you happen to be lonely. Can you deny it? You cannot. Yes . . . in Sweden, where I come from, it's even worse. Besides, I speak Norwegian all right. I've been out with Norwegian ships for many years. I came here on a Norwegian ship. Then I fell down into the hold and broke my leg and had to stay behind at the hospital here. And in the meantime the Norwegian ship left, with another man in my place. So that was that. They paid the bill, they certainly did that, but in any case . . . I have work for the time being. I roll the barrels along the quay down here. It's enough to keep body and soul together. But there's nothing like a life on the ocean wave. Arriving at new ports. Beautiful women with black eyes just waiting for you. Nothing like being at home either, with a cute little wife. Damned miserable and depressing, that's what it is.'

Mrs Katinka stood listening to all this. But she's stupid

in many ways, and she was probably a bit drunk already. She started a conversation going too. She said, 'Can't you go back to sea again?' As if it was of any importance what a fellow like that did with himself!

'Women always ask those kinds of questions. Well, begging your pardon, but that's how it is. To sea again? When all that tonnage is laid up the world over, or nearly all? There aren't any ships on the sea any more, thanks to the blasted war. As long as the war was on we earned plenty, let me tell you, risking our wretched lives. But no sooner is it over . . . It doesn't "pay" any more, that's what they say now. They ought to try hanging about here themselves, the bigwigs who caused all this misery. The German emperor first, of course.'

And still Katinka made no move to go, if you please. She stayed, and said, 'But you must have some friends?'

'Sure, especially on pay-day. Then you're quite a hero. Nobody's sitting at home waiting to see that money, so all it's good for is to be drunk away. Don't get me wrong, they're good lads in their fashion. But they have their homes and their wives. They ask me home now and again. But I'm too proud, you see. I don't want to be a nuisance. This spring, too, so damned light. What's one to do with oneself on evenings like this? Saturday evening on top of it all, when work stops at one o'clock?'

Katinka had no answer to this. Not one that could be heard, at least. But neither did she go. It was incredible, but . . .

In the shop they were beside themselves. Was she really going to stay chatting with that fellow? She hadn't the time, and it simply wasn't respectable. She had almost got away too.

Behind the door Bowler Hat said, 'It's as if you weren't human. I'll end going with girls again. Getting myself some drunk, filthy, stupid girl. Who else?! I've tried coming here in the evenings for company. But you have to be at least a barber or something of the sort to be taken notice of. It's as if they hated you, every man jack of them. What did you say?'

'Oh, nothing.'

And Mrs Stordal had said nothing. But she went on listening to this nonsense, this immoral chatter. Instead of going home to sew.

'Devilish bad luck my wife died, at any rate,' continued the fellow. 'Since then . . . She was a fine little woman. She kept me in order. Cute too. A cute little woman.'

Suddenly he opened the door a crack, so that the ladies on the other side rushed in a fright each to her own corner. At the same moment the revolving door started to move and they heard him say, 'Shhh, somebody's coming. Sit down.'

He went back to sit at the table. And would you believe it, Mrs Katinka sat down too, at her table. Just as if ordered to do so. Gracious heavens!

The person who came in was Mrs Breien. She entered in that brisk manner in which she does everything, enthusiastic as she is. But then she does have a lot to see to. There's always someone for her to help, if nothing else.

She was carrying a rather large, bulky parcel. She paused in the middle of the room and looked about her. 'Katinka – I mean Mrs Stordal – isn't here by any chance?'

Mrs Breien talks in a high treble.

'She's in the parlour, Mrs Breien,' said Mrs Krane, which was only too true.

'In there? Thank you so much. I'm in such a hurry. I've been looking for her all over town.'

And Mrs Breien fussed with her parcel through the sliding door. It wasn't easy with only one hand, but she managed it. Larsen, who hurried to help her, got there too late. Mrs Breien does everything so quickly.

She hesitated for a moment at the sight of that dreadful

23

Bowler Hat, then put her parcel down on the table in front of Mrs Stordal. Quietly, but audibly, and emphasizing every word, she said, *'What are you thinking of, Katinka?'*

'Constance,' began Mrs Stordal, as if about to explain herself. But how could she explain herself? Everything was about as bad as it could be, and she got no further.

Mrs Breien intended to talk quietly on account of that unwelcome man who sat there having nothing to do with the affair, but she spoke quite loudly now and again, and lengthily, and without pausing for breath, for that's how Mrs Breien is. She means well. She said, 'I think I'll sit down for a moment, my dear. How I've run after you!'

She sniffed at Mrs Stordal's glass. 'Port? Ugh! And you drink that in the middle of the day? I must undo my coat a little, I'm *so* hot. Now look here, Katinka, you mustn't make things too difficult for us; we really do want to help you. We can't take the responsibility for anything any more, my dear. Mrs Buck has been waiting for you at home since one o'clock. Torsen phoned and asked if you were at my house; she thought she had seen you going in that direction. Nothing's ready for fitting either, I was given to understand. And that's a frightful shame, you know. A lady like Mrs Buck won't be satisfied with that sort of thing. She can afford to buy her clothes anywhere she likes, abroad even. If she's decided to give you this order, you *must* do your best. Otherwise it makes things impossible for us who are trying to find you work, you see. Now go home this minute and apologize to her nicely – you'll have to find some excuse or other – and give her as much of a fitting as you can. And then get down to some sewing. You'll have to sit up a couple of nights for once. If you must, you must. You're not to let anyone down this time, there's far too much at stake.'

'For once,' repeated Mrs Stordal bitterly. As if *she* had any reason to be bitter. Stays up wasting her time night after night, sometimes without the slightest necessity for it.

But Mrs Breien is splendid. All she said, patiently and

politely, was, 'Plenty of people have to work hard these days, Katinka. It seems to me we hear nothing but how miserably people live. And there's unemployment everywhere. Those who have something to do ought to be glad. Now go straight home. Then you can tell yourself afterwards that you did what you could. You know what I mean. I believe Mrs Buck is kind. If she takes an interest in you we've gained a lot. You must think of *my* position, if nothing else.'

Mrs Breien spoke the last words with particular emphasis. Then she pointed at the parcel. 'Just a bit of mutton stew, dear. We had it ourselves yesterday. I brought it with me because I thought you wouldn't have time to prepare any proper dinner today. I warmed it up a bit too, in case you wanted to eat it straightaway. So you'll have something for the children's dinner. It's *so* good and filling. There'll be enough for tomorrow as well. You know I'd much rather invite you home to me, but there's Mr Breien. He's a bundle of nerves these days. And it would take up too much of your time, to be honest.

'You must do this, Katinka. You know we only want what's best for you,' added Mrs Breien, warmly persuasive.

'You're a good person, Constance,' said Mrs Stordal slowly. The tone of her voice was curious. If it had not been out of the question, you might almost have thought she meant something completely different.

'Oh, poof.' Mrs Breien wasn't one to parade her helpfulness. And she was superior to the tone used by someone who is half drunk.

It was then that Bowler Hat interrupted the conversation. Yes, *that* was really the beginning of the whole affair.

'Watch out for *her*,' he said to Katinka.

Imagine, the impertinence!

Naturally Mrs Breien took not the slightest notice. And whatever Mrs Stordal *did*, she *said* nothing. Not at that point.

25

But Bowler Hat persisted. 'Don't let her get a hold on you. All she'll do is turn you into a pauper. What I mean is, she'll make you *feel* like a pauper. And then you're *finished*.'

'We'll go now, shall we, Katinka?' said Mrs Breien calmly, ignoring this impudent person. 'I'm going your way. Come along.'

'If you let her decide, there'll be nothing left of you.' Bowler Hat got to his feet and advanced across the room. 'People like her can turn the lot of us into miserable beggars.'

Imagine saying that about kind Mrs Breien! He turned to her and said, 'Leave the poor woman alone. Can't you see she's tired?'

And he went over to Mrs Stordal and said in that low, one might almost be tempted to say melodious voice, if it were not so ridiculous, and offensive and bold into the bargain, 'May I offer you something? Something you'd fancy? What about a little wine? The wine you've just been drinking? And then you can go on listening to me for a while? You mustn't stop listening yet, you understand so well. I expect you know too how it feels to be lonely? Loneliness – it's worse than the cold. And the cold is terrible. You'll be doing a kindness to a poor devil. I'll order the wine.'

It could no longer be denied that he was the one Katinka was listening to. She stood staring helplessly in front of her, making no move to go. She even said, '*Surely* there's no need to hurry?'

'No need to hurry? You don't know what you're saying. That's precisely what we must do, hurry. Have you drunk too much again? Have you got a craving for it?' Mrs Breien was beginning to get angry. And no wonder.

'Leave her alone,' said Bowler Hat once more.

So Mrs Breien went resolutely out into the shop and shut the door behind her. 'How many glasses of wine has Mrs Stordal had?'

Larsen and Sønstegård were able to reply in unison with a clear conscience, 'Not more than one, Mrs Breien.'

'Tut, tut, tut,' clucked Mrs Krane. 'What a business!'

'She mustn't be given a drop more, do you hear?' Mrs Breien was determined now. 'Well, I'll try to get her to come with me,' she said.

With which she went back into the parlour and talked gently and kindly to Katinka. For that's how Mrs Breien is, long-suffering and reasonable. 'We *must* go, my dear. Mrs Buck's waiting. The children will be home from school at two. If they were to find you here —'

'I don't suppose I'll be here at two.'

'No, I hope not.' Mrs Breien's voice had become quite sharp. Her patience was beginning to crack, and not surprisingly.

'I've provided you with orders,' she said. 'I've provided you with Torsen to help you. And God knows, Torsen is kind, but even Torsen can't live on air, even Torsen must eat. That's another thing you should remember.'

And imagine it, Katinka laughed. A brief, utterly unprovoked little laugh. 'Even Torsen must eat,' she repeated. And laughed a second time.

As if it was funny.

Mrs Breien took it in her wise, kind manner again. 'You must understand that, Katinka.'

'Oh yes, yes.'

'You must take life as it comes. All of us have to do that.'

And Mrs Breien clearly meant a good deal by that.

But Mrs Stordal suddenly put her hand to her breast and said, 'Somebody's standing on me, bending and stretching, bending and stretching. They're trampling on my heart. The blood's trickling from it.'

She spoke pensively and with amazement, as if she really could feel it, as if she were not talking drivel at all. Then she whispered, 'Soon it will break. Somebody's

trampling on it. Soon it will break with a sigh. Then it'll
be over.'

All of them heard her, including the ladies in the shop.
They were quite close to the door.

As usual Mrs Breien was magnificently equal to the
situation. 'Now then, we mustn't get hysterical, you know.
We mustn't give up. Everyone has worries. I don't know
of anyone without worries. This really is naughty of you,
Katinka. As soon as this rush is over, everything will be
easier. But if you don't pull yourself together now, I
don't know what will happen. We'll all have to give up.'

And – guess what? Katinka went back and sat down
again, leaning on her elbows far over the table as if settl-
ing down for good. Not a word in reply, nor did she look up.

'Now, you can't stay sitting here.'

'You mean with someone like me, of course,' said that
fearful Bowler Hat.

'I'm not talking to you.'

'You don't need to. I understand you all right.'

'I'm going, Katinka.'

Mrs Breien waited a moment for an answer, was given
none, sighed and went out into the shop. She left the door
open. As if she was going to shut it, and take their feelings
into consideration! The other ladies were back in their
places; it looked better that way.

Poor Mrs Breien, who had done so much for Mrs
Katinka. She collapsed into a chair despairingly.

'Heaven help us, the children!' she managed to get out.
'That fellow . . . Mrs Stordal is actually sitting in there
with a man – talking to him and everything!'

'Of course we know that. I can't tell you how relieved I
was when I saw you coming, Mrs Breien. Tut, tut, tut. It's
so embarrassing for us, all this.'

But Mrs Breien tapped her forehead significantly.

'Surely you don't mean she's mad?' said Mrs Krane in a
horrified whisper.

'Mad or drunk. One or the other.'

'Well, it didn't happen here,' Larsen assured her. 'Who knows what she'd put away before she came here. That *this* should happen now! I can't make head or tail of it.'

From inside the parlour Bowler Hat could be heard saying, 'Now we're going to catch it. We'll tell them all to go to hell, shall we?'

And bless me if he didn't stick his head out into the shop, chewing on that everlasting cigarette butt of his. 'Half a port here. Half a *bottle*. With cookies – biscuits. And look sharp about it!'

The ladies looked at each other irresolutely.

'You can't refuse to serve me. That won't wash.'

Nobody made a move.

'Perhaps I should ask the manager himself?'

There was no point in letting the man know that Krane was not at home, that he was away at Southfjord into the bargain. Mrs Krane made a resigned gesture at Sønstegård with her knitting needle. Sønstegård disappeared, sour as as a lemon. Bowler Hat shut the door with a slam and a clatter.

'Mr Krane always has to be away when something happens,' sighed Mrs Krane helplessly. Not that there's much support to be had from him, and she knows that better than anyone else. Good at managing the café, decent and respectable, never touches a drop of liquor, but no hero. Still, a man's a man all the same. He could have shown his face, at any rate.

'The police —?'

'As long as there's no commotion, Mrs Breien —'

'I think there's a commotion, a tremendous commotion,' declared Mrs Breien with disapproval. 'And if those dresses aren't finished, *you'll* be considered responsible, Mrs Krane. It will harm your establishment.'

'Much more pleasant if we could get them to go amicably, don't you think?'

'Amicably? Two drunkards? Besides, they refuse to serve drunkards at respectable places.'

'Of course I know that.'

'Heaven help us!'

'It's not an easy matter, Mrs Breien.'

'Heaven help us, that's what I say.'

And Mrs Breien started to get things off her chest. At first quite quietly with her voice under control, but agitated as she was it soared repeatedly up into falsetto: 'There sits Katinka Stordal, a well-bred woman, the mother of two lovely children. With an individual like that. Letting everything go to rack and ruin about her. For it *is* going to rack and ruin. Nothing in the world can prevent it all going to rack and ruin.'

She deliberately raised her voice. 'Well, I'm going. I can do no more.'

She sighed, shook her head mournfully at Sønstegård who was on her way through the shop with the order, caught sight of herself in the mirror and exclaimed, 'Heaven help us!' for the third time. Mrs Breien is the sort who has no time to think about her appearance; she has so many irons in the fire for others. But that doesn't mean she has no desire to look attractive. She hastily rearranged her hair, which was really untidy, sighed once more and went.

In the meantime Sønstegård had pushed the sliding door wide open, sending it straight into the wall. She arrived in time to hear Bowler Hat say, 'Did she say drunk? Bloody bitch.'

No wonder Sønstegård was looking offended at having to serve a person like that. She left the door open behind her, obviously. Just anybody can't be allowed to shut themselves in there. There are limits.

But Mrs Stordal understood how improper it all was, in spite of everything. They heard her say, 'No, I ought to go.'

'No, you don't,' said Bowler Hat. He walked across the room, presumably taking the tray over to her. 'Look, here's your wine. It's for you. Drink up, it'll do you good.'

And bless me if he didn't shut the door again, sliding it along even faster than Sønstegård had, if that were possible.

What impertinence! Mrs Krane could at least have said something about that door. But all she did was look unhappy and position herself to listen.

In a trice all three of them were listening. In case matters got out of control in there. And as long as no other customers came in . . .

'You're not drunk,' said Bowler Hat. 'You're unhappy. And no wonder.'

'*Skål*,' said Katinka. So she must have been drunk.

She said it somewhat despairingly and helplessly, but still . . .

'Travelling round the world . . . must be . . . must at least be —?' she went on, fumbling and embarrassed, as if she didn't quite know what to say.

And well might she be embarrassed. Serve her right, the way she got herself mixed up in this.

'Yes indeed, there's fresh air, a wide sky, sometimes it's boring, sometimes full of variety, beautiful women in every port. Some of them don't bother much about the women. Well, apart from one thing, of course. When that's over and done with they don't care a rap for them. But I appreciate women, I appreciate being with them in other circumstances too. I appreciate their company.

'Of course, you have to rough it at sea,' he said, changing his tone. 'But still it's better than hanging about here. Yet I ought to be thankful, with the situation as it is, especially for seamen. I have buddies who're begging from door to door at home in Sweden, so I can't grumble.'

The fellow even started on his family affairs, as if he and Katinka were old acquaintances. 'I have a little girl. At home in Gävle.'

'Then you do have somebody,' said Katinka. She still sounded unsure of what to say.

'Nonsense!'

He can't have meant to sound as impolite as he did, for immediately afterwards the man said, in that voice which really did have something strange about it, especially when you heard it but couldn't see him, 'I'm sorry. I know you mean well, but surely you know yourself it's nonsense. Young people. Drink up now. If you'd like more, you shall have it.'

No doubt that Katinka did as she was told. There was the clink of a glass against a plate. To be blunt, she sounded a bit husky when she said, 'But she's fond of you, isn't she?'

At any rate she was earnest, as drunk people are. As if it was really important for her to find out whether this girl was fond of her father or not.

'Oh, maybe she likes me. But it's my in-laws, you see, who look after her. And my mother-in-law will never forgive me, because the child arrived sooner than it ought to have done. She blames me for my wife's death too. My wife got consumption, and she says it was because I didn't do well enough, so that she was forced to work and take on more than she could stand. But my wife never said so. She wasn't like that. She forgave me everything. Oh, I did do things I shouldn't, but so have we all, I suppose. My daughter's at the age when her friends are all that matters. Besides, I haven't done so well by her either. I haven't paid for her as I ought, you see. But here I am confessing my sins to you. *Skål.*'

'But I've paid,' said Katinka absent-mindedly.

And she had in a way too, even though it always misfired. But imagine saying so to that stranger!

'And still you're lonely. I expect you're always lonely. But there, you see, it's all the same whatever you do. You might just as well not bother. They don't care a damn for us; all they think about is themselves. Besides, young people are unkind. They enjoy hurting. Haven't you noticed that? We disgust them.'

What a lot of preaching! And that stupid Katinka blurted out in agreement, 'Oh, yes!'

'They think they're marvellous just because they're young, you see. They can't stand anyone else getting old. We need plenty of money and power and social position to

keep our end up against them. If we haven't got it —!
And even if we did have it . . . They're *arrogant* because
they're young, you see.'

And there sat Bowler Hat inciting Mrs Katinka, to put it
bluntly. Mrs Katinka, who was quite impossible already.
Larsen looked at Sønstegård and Sønstegård at Mrs Krane.
Mrs Krane shook her head in despair.

'You have to keep your mouth shut when you're with
them,' he said. 'Feed them and all that, but don't say too
much.'

'Don't say too much.'

Now she was imitating him, too. Her voice sounded as if
something that had been on her mind for a long time had
now been confirmed. Talk about a situation!

'That's gospel truth, that is,' Bowler Hat assured her.
'You can count on it. No questions either.'

'Questions? No, of course not.'

'They don't even suspect that they'll get old themselves
one day.'

'I don't care about them any more.'

Katinka was suddenly speaking loudly, as if she had to
shout down someone. 'I can't do anything for them, anyway. I've run around after them like a little dog,' she
added angrily.

Bowler Hat muttered something. It was impossible to
hear what, but it sounded as if someone was knocking his
fist against the table.

'Did you ever?' said Mrs Krane, clearly sunk in some
train of thought.

'Hush!' exclaimed Larsen and Sønstegård. 'Let's hear a
bit more, can't we?'

And hear they did. Katinka was talking nonsense with a
vengeance now. 'Mother love,' she said. 'They talk about
mother love. As if it can put up with anything. But it's a
myth, a convenient myth. What do most people get from
their children? Patronizing contempt. Pity, when they
feel a higher emotion. It kills love, every kind of love.'

33

'That's true.'

'My children can't stand me, let me tell you.'

'How many do you have, Katinka?'

'Two.'

'Two? Just the right number to gang up against you.'

'It's not quite like that either . . .'

Goodness, how intimate they were getting. Katinka and *that* fellow! And talking about that sort of thing, dragging the children into it. Mrs Stordal had sunk lower than anyone had suspected. Still, she had been a respectable woman once, one of the loveliest young girls.

'I tried to do my best, you see. But that's just stupid. You get nothing in return. They despise you for it.'

'Why do you give a damn about them?'

'I don't give a damn about them. That's what I'm doing here. Do you know about the kind of love that's like anger, it's so powerless? Do you?'

'Lord, yes.'

'This Christmas, for instance. Those cold, critical stares at everything. The silence, the oppressive atmosphere. I had done all I could. Flew all over the place. Begged. Ran into debt. Into still more debt. It's never enough, never sufficient. It's no good explaining yourself. What is there to explain? You can't do more than your best, can you? D'you think I'm going to sit there one more Christmas? Like a criminal? A person who hasn't done her duty? No! No! No!'

'Here, take a swig. It helps. For a while, at least. Afterwards —'

'Afterwards?'

'Afterwards maybe we'll hit on something. A way out —'

'A way out. Yes . . .'

'Hush, now. We're not there yet. You don't have to tell me, my dear, which way your thoughts were running just now when I came in. I've been around long enough to understand that. *Skål!* Now we'll drink to the fact that it's not going to happen this time.'

34

The ring of glasses on plates.

'It's just that I'm so tired,' said Katinka.

Children and drunkards will tell you the truth. Both Larsen and Sønstegård admitted later that at that point they were almost afraid of more customers coming. For it *was* exciting to listen to Mrs Katinka, who scarcely ever gave you an answer in the normal run of affairs, sitting there giving rein to her tongue. Even though it was so dreadful to hear her gossiping like that about her own children. Throwing them to the wolves, you might almost call it.

And even though it was all a lot of nonsense.

What else could you call it?

Her voice, which had sunk to a low mumble for a while, was audible again : '. . . sometimes, when you're feeling – well, a bit lonely – it can slip out . . . you make suggestions . . . to get a little friendliness, a little . . . tenderness. It's a great weakness, a great lack of pride. And you get the reply you deserve : "Leave me alone, Mother – there's a new cowboy film on next week." "But Mother – a Lloyd steamer has collided with a fishing boat in the Channel." '

'Yes. I'm afraid it's never any good appealing to them.'

'And what have I to do with them really? People I know nothing about, don't understand, with their strange gestures, strange laughter. Oh, that strange laughter. You understand, I've wanted so much to be a mother to them too, I remember so well how it was when they were small. Even now that they're big I often have a desire to put my hand out and pat them, simply because I can't find the words, I don't know what to say. That's what animals do, after all – they lick their young – it must be because they can't speak. But people have so many new ideas nowadays. The things we believed to be most natural seem to be quite wrong.'

Whatever could Mrs Katinka have meant by that? Nothing probably. It was simply drunken chatter. Sentimentality. On the other hand it was alarming that she should suddenly sound as if she were about to fall asleep. She even yawned.

'That *would* be the last straw,' whispered Mrs Krane.

'We'll have to carry her out soon,' said Sønstegård grimly.

'Gracious heavens! And all those dresses. And Mr Krane in Southfjord.'

But Katinka went on with her chatter, persistently as if half asleep, and yet quite clearly.

'When they were small I sometimes thought, if I were to die, what would they remember about me? The coat I wore, a brooch perhaps, or a scarf? Not my face. For that *is* the way we remember people who died when we were children, and *now* – if I were to die now it would be my faults, the times when I was inadequate —'

'Let's finish the bottle. This won't do.'

'Besides, we can be killed by words. Some little thing is said, and we begin to die . . . go to pieces —'

'Yes, that's true enough.'

'But when I feel I can't take it any longer? When I've become spiteful and wicked and vulgar and petty, then surely I might just as well —?'

'Of course, you damn well should. Exactly what I've always thought. Just leave. But not by jumping overboard. You must have something else in life besides them?'

'To be forced to let them see I'm so ugly, so —'

'The children, you mean? Oh, them – they don't even *see* you.'

'Oh yes, they see me. And it disgusts them. You get thin-skinned, like – like in a love affair. You withdraw into yourself at the slightest criticism. It's difficult, let me tell you, to keep love, any kind of love. That's a question of money, too.'

'Now then, have a swig and forget all about them.'

'Tut, tut, tut,' said Mrs Krane. 'We must go and sit down,' she added. 'It looks so dreadful, our standing here. Customers might come in.'

Unwillingly Larsen and Sønstegård went back to the napkins. Mrs Krane was already in position with her knitting. It was almost coffee time. Odd that no one had come in already.

'It may be more important to keep order among the customers we have,' sulked Sønstegård. 'Get them out in time. If they're to be allowed to go on talking nonsense in there . . .'

She did not finish the sentence. It remained hanging in the air, heavy with unpleasantness, unresolved and threatening.

'Funny, the things drunk people say,' mused Larsen.

'Funny? Yes, I suppose so, if you find that sort of thing funny. Tragic, in my opinion.'

'Tut, tut, tut,' clicked Mrs Krane impatiently. Why couldn't those two hold their tongues? Then she might have been able to hear something from where she was sitting.

Outside, a woman walked past the windows.

'Elise Oyen!' exclaimed Larsen and Sønstegård in unison.

'Surely she's not coming here?' Mrs Krane began knitting her pullover so violently that she dropped several stitches at once.

'Why should that matter? We're open to everyone, everyone respectable I mean.'

Just like Larsen to make a remark like that.

'She's gone into Berg and Fure's,' she said, craning her neck. 'Oh dear, isn't she good-looking?'

'Good-looking? Oh yes, when she's all dolled up,' said Sønstegård.

'You're right. More dolled up than good-looking really.'

Larsen sounded relieved. 'But the bank doesn't close until four,' she added, uneasy again.

'Pooh, that one pleases herself. They all seem to be at her beck and call.'

'They do, don't they? I wonder how things are between her and Stordal these days?'

'God knows. She flirts with so many.'

'Yes, indeed.' Larsen's voice dropped several tones from indignation. 'Yes, that's for sure.'

Mrs Krane gave a warning cough.

The revolving door was set spinning. In came Solicitor Buck and his wife. While they were still in the doorway Mrs Buck could be heard saying, 'Indeed, and it's gone too far now, Gottfred.'

'Agreed, agreed.'

Mrs Krane put down her knitting and stood waiting politely for their order.

'Let's go in there,' said Buck, making for the parlour.

'I'm sorry, I'm afraid it's occupied, Mr Buck.' Mrs Krane spoke in a falsetto tone, from sheer nervousness.

'Occupied?' Buck was clearly unaccustomed to anyone obstructing his plans. He raised his eyebrows as far as they would go.

'I'm afraid so, Mr Buck. But what about this? Isn't this a nice table? Such a pleasant view, I always think.' Mrs Krane indicated the window table where Larsen and Sønstegård were sitting, while they hastily moved away, taking their paper napkins with them.

Without getting involved in the discussion, Mrs Buck settled at a table in the middle of the room. There she sat, a little on the plump side perhaps, but a lady through and through – with her Persian lamb and several diamond rings. She unbuttoned her fur coat at once and slung it over the back of the chair. Imagine, a coat like that. She already had two cream slices on her plate, and ordered coffee. 'Surely, Gottfred, it doesn't matter where we sit,' she said.

'I thought you wanted to talk to me about something.'
Solicitor Buck looked about him with displeasure and shook
his head at Larsen. He would have nothing. Larsen left
them.

'Yes, indeed I do.'

'But we can't talk here,' said Buck with annoyance. 'We
could have stayed in my office, and we'd have finished with
it by now. You get me out here to no purpose in the middle
of office hours.'

A man as busy as Mr Buck didn't like that sort of thing,
it was clear.

'I had to have a cup of coffee, indeed I did, Gottfred.
I've been sitting up there waiting for nearly an hour. And
I walked to town too. Can't we have a little music, Mrs
Krane?'

Mrs Krane went across and switched on Copenhagen
again – the waltz from *Harlequin's Millions*, not too loud.

'They won't hear when the radio's on,' said Mrs Buck.
'Besides, everyone knows about it, indeed they do. After
all, they see her out in the street.'

'She shouldn't be out in the street. She should stay home
and sew.' Buck drummed his fingers on the table.

Neither Mrs Krane, who was sitting farthest away from
the radio, nor Larsen, who was serving the coffee, could
help but hear him.

'We can't be *so* strict either, Gottfred, as to say she
shouldn't go out. Maybe she *has* to go out, to buy something or other for her sewing. You can't send someone
else to get everything, sometimes you have to go yourself.
If only she'd come home at the proper time.'

Mrs Buck was a thoroughly kind person, you could see
that. Perhaps what they said was true, that life with Buck
was sometimes a trial. He was small, curt, and bald, and
he sounded exceedingly impatient. 'Yes, yes, yes, you
mustn't take me so literally, Gudrun. You have no sense
of humour.'

'*I* have no sense of humour? How can you say such a

39

thing, Gottfred? What about all the fun we had at home, when we got engaged! And do you think this is humorous?'

But Buck was still annoyed. He looked about him for all the world as if he suspected Mrs Krane, Larsen and Sønstegård of *listening*. 'I haven't forgotten anything. But to get back to Mrs Stordal . . .'

So they *were* talking about Mrs Katinka. And there she was, sitting in the parlour – she and Bowler Hat. Talk about a situation! Of course the ladies did all they could, so as not to understand; but now one, now the other, could scarcely help hearing snatches here and there.

'You must give her an ultimatum, Gottfred. You're the person to do it, indeed you are.'

'I did give her an ultimatum, quite recently. I though I'd given her a good fright. And now she's out gallivanting again.'

'What did you do, Gottfred?'

'Sent her a letter. Told her I couldn't let it go any further, she must pay up. And before twelve o'clock on Monday. In cash, I said or else —'

'Or else, Gottfred? Come on, tell me.'

'Or else we'll clear the apartment. We'll get a lodger who *can* pay.'

'You mean you'll throw her into the street, then, Gottfred?'

'Just about, yes. She's in arrears with nine months' rent, among other things, among many other things. Well, I gave her a fortnight to pay up. I'm not inhuman.'

'When did you write this?'

'A week, ten days ago. If only she'd keep at her sewing. But she doesn't even do that.'

This was where Mrs Krane's eyes filled with tears for the first time, without her being able to explain to herself why. When people like Mrs Stordal get into such a mess there's no reason to feel sorry for them. *They're* not to be pitied, it's Mrs Krane who's foolish. Unfortunately she showed herself to be foolish more than once during all the commotion. She shouldn't be upset about it, people have said; it has to do with her age. But I wonder. She's never been able to listen to certain things without going all queer about it and getting a lump in her throat. No, sentimental, that's what she is, and always has been.

Fortunately she managed to hide her tears from Larsen and Sønstegård for the time being. They were sitting there with suitably funereal expressions, full of excitement at the same time, and pretending not to understand a thing.

Both of them looked up when Mrs Buck put down her fork despairingly, quite forgetting where she was. 'What a nitwit you can be, Gottfred! Yes indeed, what a nit-wit!'

'Whatdidyousay?' exclaimed Buck, forgetting to talk quietly too.

'Don't you see? You should have waited, at least until the ball was over. We're all of us so anxious about our dresses.'

'Don't talk so loudly,' said Buck in annoyance.

'You should have written that you had to have the money. Not a word about throwing her into the street. Where will she sit and sew then, Gottfred? Have you thought about that? In four days, if she can't pay? And she can pay only when she's delivered all those dresses – if at all.'

'Sit and sew?'

At that moment a steamer hooted out on the fjord. Mrs Krane, Larsen and Sønstegård nodded at each other and rushed to the windows. For whatever is happening you must watch the coastal express come in, especially in fine weather, white-painted and splendid, just like a foreign cruise ship.

'Hell's bells, there she comes. I can't sit here any longer.'

Buck got up. He said angrily, 'I'm sick and tired of the woman, sick of hearing about her, sick of having anything to do with her. She's cost enough, been expensive enough for me and others. People who don't learn to swim must go to the bottom, and there's nothing to be done about it. If all the rest of us who can swim are going to have to tow those who can't, the whole caboodle will end up at the bottom.'

'That's not what I mean, Gottfred,' replied Mrs Buck imperturbably. She knew Buck well, that was easy to see, and was not afraid of him. 'The steamer's still far out on the fjord.'

'She needn't have renewed the lease, while there was still time. But no, she'd manage it. And then this Mrs Breien comes interfering. Reviving something that was doomed to die of itself. That should have been allowed to die of itself. A *gifted* dressmaker! Unparalleled nonsense! Soon she'll be expecting public funds for sitting there being gifted, a grant, an artist's stipend. Why did you let yourself get involved in all this? Why didn't you order from the south as you usually do? You could all have ordered from the south, surely, every man jack of you?'

'Ordering from the south is not for everyone. But don't let's start on that. You must do something about this, Gottfred.'

'When she won't even sit at home and look after her business like the rest of us? I'll be damned if I will.'

'Yes indeed, you must do something. There'll be a proper revolt in the town.'

'Then there'll have to be a revolt. Have you finished your coffee? If not, you'd better stay.'

Buck turned to go, but paused. 'Damnation, there's that lot coming now. I haven't the time, so help me —'

'Take it easy, Gottfred. It's only the young and the beautiful. I'm sure you can spare the time. And now you'll be able to hear for yourself.'

A group of young women had gathered outside, chattering loudly, obviously about to enter. They sounded like a flock of birds.

God Almighty, thought Mrs Krane. She hurried over to

the shelves, as close to the sliding door as possible, and seemingly began tidying up there while she listened to the couple in the parlour. She would never be rid of them if people were to keep coming in like this. And these, of all people. If only it had been just anybody. The wives could have gone down to take a look at the coastal steamer first. They usually did.

At first she could hear nobody but Mrs Buck: 'Now then, Gottfred, the first thing you do at the office, the very first thing, is to send a note. If you don't, who will be the one to suffer all the consequences, do you think? It'll be me, you'll see.'

'Hush,' said Buck.

And what Mrs Krane was listening for so tensely was given the chance of reaching her. The voice – that voice which could have made anyone feel a bit odd if it had come from someone else, and which was clearly only meant for Mrs Katinka – said: 'I'd like to give you something. A flower? Won't you let me give you a flower? I saw some beautiful ones in the flower shop on my way here. I saw some *bellis*. Aren't *bellis* beautiful, don't you think? Then you'd have something to look at tomorrow. It's Sunday. And Sunday's the most difficult day, isn't it?'

'Sunday's the most difficult day,' repeated Katinka like a parrot, mimicking his Swedish accent. A glass clinked repeatedly against a plate.

'That's when you're left alone as on no other day. That's when they all go off, each and every one, to enjoy themselves. Yet you feel you ought to be able to enjoy yourself too.'

'*Bellis*? What a beautiful name! It must be Latin.'

'God knows. That's what we call them in Sweden. Though a lot of people call them English daisies.'

'Oh yes, daisies.'

'That's right, daisies, daisies,' drivelled Bowler Hat. Then he said in a completely different voice, 'You thought of doing a bolt this time. I understand that much, though

43

I'm a simple man. You needed a glass or two to give you courage, didn't you? But you're not going to let them drive you overboard are you? Not you.'

Katinka had no answer to that, none that Mrs Krane could hear. And surely she couldn't have thought of going and drowning herself, with all those orders, she the mother of two children besides? Nobody did that sort of thing in this town.

Suddenly it struck Mrs Krane that that sort of thing was not just written up in the paper about people in other places. Greve the chemist had taken Prussic acid in the cellar of his shop, though that had happened a long time ago, and he was even scolded at his graveside by Mr Pio, the curate. A person who takes his own life, Pio had said, is a great sinner. Many considered this rather severe. And Iversen the tailor, who had such a spiteful wife, had *walked* out into the sea until it went over his head, and he never came up again, even though it was ebb tide and the sea was far out. People who saw him from the Stoppenbrink Quay waved their arms and shouted and tried to run after him, but it was no use because of the distance. That had been a long time ago too, but still . . .

A drowned body! There is nothing so horrible as a drowned body! Mrs Krane had seen one once at Southfjord, a fisherman who had been washed ashore. She had been afraid of the dark for a long time afterwards. Now that she thought about it, it was the third time Bowler Hat had brought up the subject in there. Mrs Katinka had not contradicted him, and she had been given four days' notice to quit . . .

It was then that Mrs Krane became frightened. According to her own story, so frightened that it gave her quite a turn, and she didn't really know what she was doing any more. She used this as an excuse. It seemed to her as if anything could happen all of a sudden, unpredictably. And should she be glad or sorry that this scandalous couple were still sitting in the parlour? She was utterly confused.

44

As she stood there she became aware of Buck again – 'I think I have been lenient,' he said.

'Yes indeed, you've been more than kind, Gottfred. But now there's no choice but to be kind a little while longer.'

'I've been more than patient with this woman. She's made me look quite ridiculous.'

'You ridiculous? Oh, come now.'

'People who are too kind get laughed at sooner or later. She has orders for several dresses for the ball, hasn't she? And she'll get at least thirty *kroner* per dress?'

'If the style's a bit complicated, yes.'

'But surely ball dresses *are* complicated? That's just when you do want this and that from head to foot, isn't it? Frills and furbelows. Even I can see that a dress like that must cost more—'

'We don't have furbelows nowadays, Gottfred.'

'No, no. Something else, then. What I'm trying to say is that a trained dressmaker can surely make about three dresses a week? If she has to live by it? A dressmaker who sits and sews, and doesn't go running about all over the place. And who even has help? Three dresses, ninety *kroner*. If she brings ninety *kroner* to me on Monday, we'll see. It's a drop in the ocean, but there you are. Besides, a half-divorced woman like that, not quite respectable even – she has her little drinking bouts – has to be held by the scruff of the neck so that you can get what you can out of her. I bought that house on the basis of the rent it brings in. I have to abide by the contracts.'

'Quite so, Gottfred, quite so.'

The revolving door whirled at top speed. Several of the young wives of the town streamed in, all talking at once. They are all equally long-legged and fair-haired, equally well-dressed and well-groomed, equally loud-voiced. Except for Mrs Berg Junior, who's almost too quiet.

Had she not known them since their childhood, Mrs

Krane would probably have difficulty distinguishing the one from the other, so similar are their hair styles and clothes. The most stylish, most good-looking and most elegant are Mrs Fosnes and in particular Mrs Settem – who looks like a model in a foreign fashion magazine, or a film star. But then, she's newly married, and has been south every spring and autumn since her confirmation.

Mrs Berg Junior would look attractive too, if she were a little more vivacious. But her temperament tells against her. She just sits and looks innocent.

Normally Mrs Krane would have greeted them all warmly. It was pleasant that they came at this time practically every day. They gave the place such a nice atmosphere. Continental is the word, perhaps? But when you were so to speak hiding Katinka Stordal in the parlour it was not quite so pleasant. The palms of Mrs Krane's hands began to get moist.

As soon as they were inside the door the ladies stood there and went on chattering so excitedly that at first they did not notice the Bucks. Detached sentences buzzed in the air, and it was not at all difficult to guess what the conversation was about.

'Fancy your going to her at *all*! And with things you want in a hurry!'

'But she *is* the best here, unquestionably. When she wants to be. Nobody understands my figure as she does.'

'She's better than the Oslo stores, let me tell you. Her cut—'

'But if it isn't ready for a fitting on Monday at the latest—'

'What is one to do then? Go to Mrs Stenestø and become short-waisted? No thank you.'

'If only she'd keep on the rails till the ball was over.'

'Yes, poor thing.'

'Poor thing? All she's got to do is look after her business. That's what Konrad says too.'

'Look, we must talk this over, come to some agreement.'

Mrs Krane could wait no longer for what she knew was coming. She had to prevent it if possible. She fluttered among the tables. 'Here perhaps? You'll sit comfortably here. We can put two of the tables together.'

'But you know we always sit in the parlour, Mrs Krane. It's *our* parlour!'

'I'm sorry, unfortunately it's engaged.'

'Engaged? Oh, what a nuisance! It's not usually engaged at this time of day.'

'I'm afraid so.'

With trembling hands Mrs Krane moved the flower vases off the tables and then back on to them again.

'Do you feel ill, Mrs Krane?'

'I? No, I'm quite all right.'

'I thought you were looking a bit poorly.'

Fortunately several of the wives had begun talking to the Bucks. Mrs Krane breathed more easily.

'My dear, you must excuse us. We were so excited, we didn't even notice anyone was here.'

'What's the important subject under discussion? We're bursting with curiosity.' Buck adopted the fatherly tone he usually employed to attractive young women. 'Come and join us, since the other room's occupied.'

'Thank you, but there are so many of us—'

'Put another table next to ours, Miss Sønstegård, if you will.'

'What we're talking about really does concern the whole town.'

'But not a solicitor, surely?' said the quiet voice of Mrs Berg Junior. For a moment, everyone looked at her in astonishment.

'You'd be surprised how much there is that concerns me, Mrs Berg.'

'Would I?'

But nobody pays any attention to Mrs Berg Junior.

'We're talking about one of the dressmakers, the best one in town when she puts her mind to it, but utterly hopeless

47

when you have to do business with her,' volunteered another source succinctly and informatively.

'Oh indeed, oh indeed? In that case my wife will probably be interested. Now, what's it all about? Are we all comfortable?'

The scraping of chairs had died away, everyone had found somewhere to sit, everyone was talking at once except for Mrs Berg, who had been silenced, and Mrs Buck. Leaning back in her chair against that wonderful fur coat, she awaited the course of events. Her mouth was set in a queer expression; her hand with the diamond rings was playing with her coffee spoon.

Larsen had quietly turned off the radio. Nobody was paying any attention to it any more. Every loud assertion that rose above the general murmur could be heard with exceptional clarity and struck Mrs Krane to the quick.

'She *can* do a bad job, though.'

'Goodness, of course she can, when she doesn't bother.'

'But she doesn't take anything when she doesn't want to bother. Sometimes she simply says "no".'

'One thing at a time, Ladies. This actually does interest me too. I gather this dressmaker is very competent when she wants to be?'

'Good heavens, yes. What about that blue dress of mine last year? And the terracotta-coloured one Nusse had? And Lillemor's brown suit?'

'An important event is almost upon us. As I understand it, the fate of the town hangs on this one dressmaker?'

'Absolutely, there's no question about it. You've hit the nail on the head, Mr Solicitor.'

'I know people who've had to fetch their material, all ready cut out, and take it home again. She'd kept them waiting for weeks.'

'She has spells when she's quite impossible. I'm not sure that everything they say about her is true, mind you. But now she *must* pull herself together.'

'As long as she hasn't taken on too much.'

'That's her affair. And it was Mrs Breien—'

'Asta, you really did have a fitting the other day. Did you see anything of my dress? Flowered georgette?'

'There are pieces of material all over the place up there. It's impossible to tell whose they are. You all know that. None of it looked anywhere near finished.'

'Oh, why didn't I order from the south? She *has* taken on too much.'

'But after all, it's her living. And all she has to do is work. But no, she's out wandering about in broad day-light — she'd already been out a couple of hours when I phoned.'

'I saw she had help in the workroom.'

'One person. Marie Torsen. She needs at least ten.'

'Yes, goodness gracious, as if one was enough.'

'It was Torsen who said she was out. I don't think she meant to tell me, but it slipped out. It's not easy to find excuses all the time. Poor Torsen, it's not her fault.'

'And I've even paid her in advance.'

'Are you crazy? In that case you haven't a hope. No, I've said, not one *øre*, Mrs Stordal, before the dress is delivered. She always starts talking about the rent and the bills and that sort of thing. But then it can take months. That's when you have to fetch your material back.'

Buck had taken out a notebook and was writing in it. It looked as if he was making calculations and adding up. 'What does she ask, Ladies? The exact amount?'

'She insists on thirty.'

'I got it down to twenty, even though the style was rather complicated, a bit of flouncing and so on. And not an easy material. Chiffon. I couldn't give more, I said, in times like these.'

Buck noted it all down.

'We heard you had ordered your dress there too, Mrs Buck?'

'This time I did, yes indeed. Usually I get them from Oslo.'

'Are you sure she really is the best?' Buck did not look up; he was still writing in his notebook.

'Surely there's no comparison, is there?' said Mrs Buck calmly. And Mrs Settem, newly married, and since that event a shade too exquisite, a shade too prone to dreamy, becoming poses, assured them, 'I looked like a barrel in what I got from the south last year. No, when she bothers—'

'I'd have thought she'd bother for you.'

'It ought to be a delight to make clothes for you, Madame. But it's too bad, when she really *is* good at her job. I don't understand it at all, she ought to be able to earn well enough — thirty *kroner* a dress and the leading dress-maker in town. She ought to be able to deliver, let's see, at least three a week, perhaps four. Of course I don't understand these things, but I notice the other dressmakers here; they seem to manage, without being the best. Humph, people said everything would be splendid when she went to Trondheim or wherever it was to learn – for further training, as they say. I don't understand it at all, some people never seem to strike anchor.'

Buck replaced his book. 'It ought to be possible to get her to do her work,' he said curtly.

'Do you know her, Mr Solicitor?' It was Mrs Berg Junior again, in that dispirited voice of hers that never catches anyone's attention.

'Had a little to do with her, yes. Purely business.'

'Goodness, have you?'

'Send her a note, Gottfred. Write what I told you. And soon, yes indeed.'

'I expect I shall manage it, Gudrun. I'm used to handling people.'

'Imagine, if *you* could bring her to her senses, Mr Solicitor. What a surprise that would be! So many of us would be grateful to you.' Mrs Settem adopted another attractive pose, inclining forward her lovely young face which, as Lydersen says, looks so newly kissed. She knows how to move, that woman.

'It will be sufficient if *you* are grateful, Madame.'

'We must go, Gottfred. Weren't you the one who was waiting for the steamer? It's moored at the quay already.'

'Rely on me, Ladies.'

'Yes indeed, they're putting down the gangplank, Gottfred.'

'Dear Mr Solicitor, fancy your coming to the rescue!'

'My vocation in life is to come to the rescue. I have been fortunate enough to rescue not a few people. Not always as charming as—'

'You haven't the time, Gottfred.'

'I'm coming, I'm coming.'

Buck made his bow to the assembled company. The ladies replied with a chorus of good-byes.

During all this it had not been possible for Mrs Krane to keep abreast of what was going on in the other room. Talk, the clink of china, the striking of matches, had formed a protective wall round the couple inside.

What if they decided to come out this minute! Scenes were not in her line, catastrophes even less. Katinka, rushing perhaps straight into the sea before anyone could prevent her, sinking to the bottom and floating up again as a drowned corpse – oh no! It's deep at the quayside, the water was winter-cold still, and nobody besides the young boys can swim here in town. They go to World's End in the summer and practise where it's shallow.

It was possible that Bowler Hat might be able to swim, but . . .

A wild notion of getting Katinka quietly out of the window of the parlour and piloted straight home had to be rejected as too fantastic. No, it was better for them to stay where they were for the time being. Ugh, how malicious Sønstegård was looking!

'You'll see, Buck will manage it,' the wives were telling each other.

'As long as he doesn't treat her too harshly.' That was Mrs Berg Junior again.

'Oh come. You have to be a bit harsh sometimes. That's what Konrad says too, kind as *he* is. The world is best served with a little harshness, he says. Without it you get nowhere.'

'Heavens, that's true,' said someone who was not Mrs Berg. 'But to change the subject. My dears, I'd *love* to come down here and dance one evening. They say it's *such* fun, you've no idea.'

'I'd never get my husband to do that, not in this world. They're rather a peculiar crowd, aren't they?'

Isn't that what I've told Mr Krane, thought Mrs Krane, who had her ears cocked in the wives' direction for a while.

'Mrs Oyen and suchlike – and Lydersen—'

'Now then, careful with names.'

The voices dropped, but Mrs Krane heard : 'They say he dances divinely, let me tell you.'

'Let's agree on a day to meet for lunch down here again. It was such a success last time.'

'Goodness yes, do you remember the look on my husband's face when we walked in?'

'What about mine?'

'And mine? They thought they were going to have the place to themselves. Lunch in the city, as they say. To save time. But in that case we're going to lunch in the city too. Blowed if I'm going to stay at home eating a cheese sandwich while he sits here and orders lobster mayonnaise.'

'Or steak. Steak tartare?'

'Is there anything as dull as porridge? Or fried-up potatoes? But you can't let anything go to waste in times like these. Konrad—'

'Ugh, yes. No, it is nice here. For all the world like a little bit of Oslo.'

'Well, let's say Trondheim. But they've arranged things

well here. They serve the food so nicely. If they could bring themselves to alter the parlour as well, make it look a bit functional in there. I love functional design. With cactuses, you know. Think how it used to be.'

'I agree with those who want to keep the parlour as it is. D'you remember how we always went in there as children? It was almost mysterious. For this place *was* a bit mysterious. None of our mothers came here to *eat* cakes, they only fetched them. And how large the cream slices were. Only seven øre apiece.'

'Don't talk so loud, you two.'

'We're just having a pleasant chat.'

'All the same . . .'

Father-in-law's time, thought Mrs Krane. If only Mr Krane would make up his mind to have a functional parlour, we'd get only the best customers. I've said it all along. It's amazing what a difference the décor makes.

Suddenly she noticed someone walking past the window, close to the window-pane, and tut-tutted despairingly. She made violent signs to Larsen and Sønstegård with her knitting needle that they were to act as if nothing was the matter, whatever happened. They had seen him too.

'Has he found some money?' asked Sønstegård.

'Saturday, you know.'

'It was Saturday a week ago too. He wasn't here then.'

'Look at him. Frisky as a newly divorced husband.'

'Be quiet with you.'

It was Stordal, the master-builder, his overcoat unbuttoned and his hat on the back of his head. He did indeed look frisky. He's handsome, in spite of his fifty years, with plain, strong features and something naïvely good-natured about him. Some people say he's over-emotional and sentimental – when they don't actually call him affected. But of course that's an exaggeration. And he's quite capable of being firm, harsh even.

He took off his hat, he's a polite man. A couple of the ladies returned his greeting, a little distrait, a little vaguely. But Mrs Berg Junior, that innocent lamb, was actually smiling at the fellow! She'd smile at anyone. They all lowered their voices and spoke quietly for a long time.

If only they'd go, thought Mrs Krane. Then she thought : No, things might get even worse. She had guessed what was going to happen.

Quite right. Stordal was on his way towards the parlour. Mrs Krane rushed right out into the middle of the room.

'It's occupied, Mr Stordal. I know you're in the habit of sitting in there, but . . . Here's a pleasant table. Give this one by the window a wipe, if you please, Miss Larsen.'

Sønstegård sucked at her tooth so that the sound could be heard from one end of the room to the other. What was the point of trickery? Why shouldn't Stordal see what was going on? It would be all to the good if he did, since Krane was away and everything. It was Sønstegård who should have been asked to wipe over that table. That stupid girl Larsen did it without a murmur.

Stordal was not really used to being received with signs of respect. He became quite animated as a result.

'Occupied, did you say? By a private party, I suppose? There are two tables in there, after all.'

'Both tables are occupied, Mr Stordal.'

'They are not.' Sønstegård could restrain herself no longer. Surely one should stick to the truth?

Mrs Krane gave her a meaning look. 'Yes, they are.'

'Oh well, all right.' Stordal ran his hands through his hair, which he wore somewhat on the long side. Probably it's meant to look artistic; he has those kinds of pretensions. 'I'm expecting my son, you see,' he said. 'We wanted to have a little chat.' But he didn't make a fuss about it.

Nor could he very well do so. He owed a good deal for the chits he had signed, as usual. He sat down and looked out of the window.

As for Larsen, how stupid can you be? There and then she started chatting to him about subjects that could not be anything but sore points. If Sønstegård could hear what she was saying, presumably the ladies at the centre table could too. Was she trying to make herself agreeable? If so, the topic was not well chosen.

'It's the youngsters' day today, is it, Mr Stordal?'

'It's Saturday,' replied Stordal.

'Nice for youngsters to have a father like you, who takes them out with him, and all that.'

'Young people like to go out, you know.'

'How right you are! And when their mother can't manage – I mean . . .'

Here Larsen got stuck, and serve her right. But Stordal said very correctly, 'The children's mother has enough to see to.'

'That's what I mean. And now they're growing up they want a bit of fun and games.'

'Youngsters will be youngsters.'

'And men will be men. They like us to be cheerful and happy, whether we're young or old. Of course, I don't mean that Mrs Stordal's old exactly, of course she isn't . . .'

Oh, that girl Larsen! Meddling, stupid Larsen. Serve her right, let her just stand there, wanting to bite off her tongue.

'No one is old these days,' said Stordal with reserve. A handsome, fine man, Sønstegård had always said so. And that he was the one to feel sorry for.

But Larsen seemed to think she had actually made a hit. 'Isn't that so? It's just as if people didn't *get* old any more! What's it to be, then, Mr Stordal? Coffee? And cream slices? They're extra good today.'

Then Jørgen Stordal came in through the revolving door so fast that it spun round after him many times. He was

55

hot and out of breath and threw his school books down on the table.

'Well, here you are. Good afternoon, my boy.'

'Afternoon. Why aren't you sitting in the parlour?'

'It's occupied. Take your cap off. Do you see the light falling on the mountain over there, Jørgen? You don't see that anywhere else, let me tell you. Now then, we're keeping Miss Larsen waiting. What will you have?'

'Occupied? Who's there?'

'Who? Don't ask me. Some loving couple, I should think. It's the season for it. Isn't that so, Miss Larsen?'

Larsen was holding her hand over her mouth, scarlet with suppressed giggles. 'You've hit the nail on the head, Mr Stordal.' She was bubbling over with laughter.

'Was *that* so funny? It's springtime.'

'How right you are.'

'I expect we'll find out who it is, sooner or later. That sort of thing never stays secret long.'

At this point Larsen had to turn away, overcome with mirth. Everyone stared at her. Mrs Krane gave a warning cough. Stordal raised his eyebrows. If Larsen was laughing at him, by any chance, he'd thank her not to. He does take himself rather seriously.

'Dearie me, how silly I am. It was just something that came into my head. You must excuse me.' Larsen dried her tears and pulled herself together. 'What about your order, now?'

'If you've got it, I'll have a sandwich with Italian salad. And one of salt beef, and one of egg and anchovy. And one of caraway cheese. And milk.'

Jørgen finally took off his cap.

'Now then, now then, do I have to feed you, boy? You're going home to dinner, aren't you?'

Stordal spoke quietly on account of his surroundings, but Larsen could not help hearing, naturally.

'All right, if I don't get what I want I'll have to lump it,' said Jørgen sullenly.

He pulled off a handsome pair of new gloves and threw them down beside the books. He's tall and well-built, well-dressed too, there's no other word for it. But not easy. Upbringing only so-so, presumably.

And his mother was sitting in there, boozing with a man. Well, if life wasn't both tragic and peculiar, Larsen didn't know what it was. It made you get quite excited, sometimes, wondering how things were going to turn out.

Stordal signalled to her that she should get what Jørgen had ordered. No wonder he has to sign for it all the time. He's so indulgent towards those children of his. And heaven knows, perhaps the boy needed food after all.

Stordal ordered only a cup of coffee for himself, poor fellow.

Larsen went to get the order. But Sønstegård was sitting only one table away. She heard him say, 'Well, thank you very much. I had to wear knitted gloves, my boy, when I was your age. What did you pay for those?'

'Twelve seventy-five, at Berg and Fure's. Nobody in the class wears knitted gloves – none of *my* friends at any rate. It pays to buy solid stuff, you've always said so yourself. Mother thought they were expensive too, if you want to know.'

'It depends what you mean by expensive.' Stordal's voice suddenly turned harsh. He *can* be harsh, as I said. 'If it's understood that both parties share the cost, they ought not to be too expensive,' he said. 'Even though rather less handsome gloves might perhaps have done. I've always insisted that you and your sister should look decent. Tried to interfere as well, as tactfully as possible, when I considered it necessary. Things have improved in recent years, it's true. Now what did you want to talk to me about, my boy?'

'Oh, nothing.'

'Come on, what is it?'

'No, it wasn't important.'

Jørgen had become even more sullen than before. Obviously it was embarrassing for the boy, to talk like that. But how could Stordal avoid it? He can't let things slide. If he didn't keep an eye on things, goodness knows what the children would look like.

'Now, look here, you've brought me out in the middle of office hours. What's it all about? You know I'm always ready to do my utmost for you two, if it's likely to make any difference. You're my children.'

And if this didn't almost bring tears to Sønstegård's eyes! Whatever you may say about Stordal, he is a father, a good father. For her part, Sønstegård had always been on his side, and she did not regret it.

Jørgen looked about him, as if afraid that somebody might be listening. Sønstegård redoubled her efforts with the paper napkins, and began to count them.

'Come on, cough it up.'

'I've got to have a dinner jacket.'

It tumbled out of Jørgen, angrily, as if against his will.

'Heaven help us, boy. Have I a dinner jacket, I might ask?'

'Yes, you have.'

'One that's almost twenty years old, yes.'

'All my friends have dinner jackets. I've grown out of that blue suit. The others say I wear my trousers at half mast.'

'Couldn't you get them lengthened?'

'They can't be lengthened any more. They were let out their full extent ages ago.' Jørgen was talking very fast, trying to get it over and done with before Larsen came back, most likely. 'I must have something new to wear in the evening, so I might just as well get a dinner jacket. *We're* going to have a ball soon too, the school ball.'

'You'll have to talk to your mother about this.'

'I have talked to Mother.'

'What does she say?'

'Oh, can't afford it, unnecessary, can't afford such

luxury, it'll only hang in the cupboard. I must wait till I've left school.'

Stordal said nothing for a while. Then he declared, 'At your age I'd already been earning my living for a couple of years. And I had no dinner jacket. I'm a self-made man and had to live accordingly. It did me no harm. It wouldn't do you any harm either, in my opinion. But no, you had to go on with your schooling. That was your mother's idea, and I didn't stand in her way. However, now you are at school . . .'

Stordal's voice turned harsh again. And it's not to be wondered at, when you come to think about it. He said angrily, 'You must understand, my boy, after that affair with the trousers, you're not getting any more clothes from me, even if she begs and screams for them. I sent you those trousers with the best will in the world. You were walking round looking like nothing on earth in that antiquated pair . . .'

Larsen arrived, and he finished curtly, 'If the others have dinner jackets, you ought to have a dinner jacket. It should be possible to find one. Fancy having green leaves on the table already, Miss Larsen.'

'Soon be summer now, you know. People have begun taking country walks. I've heard them say the snow's melted all the way to World's End. I know someone who's found a saxifrage too. There they are, coming ashore from the steamer.'

'Yes, there they are, coming ashore.'

Larsen sat down beside Sønstegård. As if in silent agreement they folded napkins with all their might, murmuring together. Nobody could tell that they were talking sheer nonsense, quite at random.

They heard Stordal say, 'As I said, you have my support. Now then, how are things otherwise?'

'Otherwise?'

'I know you and your sister dislike saying anything. It's a trait I value. I value it highly.'

59

'But Father . . .' Jørgen looked about him uneasily.

'They can't hear. They're talking to each other.'

'Not everybody.'

'Oh yes they are.'

'You know, if only she were a little more practical,' said Jørgen unwillingly. 'After all, she must do quite well for herself.'

'It would be interesting, very interesting, to know just how well. But she probably doesn't know herself. There's a lack of certain basic qualities in her, let me tell you, as in so many women. Excellent in her way, warm-hearted, a certain amount of talent and so on. But . . . she can't really manage herself or others. It's not unthinkable that she may be saving up on the quiet, thanks to the fact that I – well, there it is. Only it wouldn't surprise me if—'

'If what?'

'Oh – if she took herself off one fine day. Left it all behind her.'

'But she can't leave,' said Jørgen. He had stopped eating.

'Women, my boy, women. You never know. If they're the kind who are never satisfied . . . There are exceptions. There *are*. But God knows, there aren't many.'

Jørgen looked about him so uneasily that something had to be done about it. Stordal *did* raise his voice now and again. Larsen said very loudly, folding energetically, 'Heavens yes, things are improving. You can't call it anything else. Dancing in the evening, toasted sandwiches, hot lunches, a revolving door, just about the whole city here between twelve and one—'

'City! Don't be so silly!'

'They call it the city, the business section down here. Just for the fun of it.'

But Stordal and Jørgen were smiling indulgently at each other. Larsen's naïvety was really amusing.

For some time it had been impossible to discover what was going on in the parlour. Mrs Krane thanked her creator – as long as they kept quiet. But it filled her with new uncertainty at the same time; you never know what two drunks may get up to. Children and drunkards will tell you the truth, they say. Suppose they had other traits in common : maybe the quieter they were, for instance, the more one should be prepared for the worst? If only Jørgen would go, she might perhaps try to get Katinka out while she was still capable of using a needle. But to let the boy see his mother in the company of that fellow – Mrs Krane was not quite heartless.

Suddenly through the buzz of conversation the portière rattled on its rod. The door slid open a crack, enough for Bowler Hat to be heard saying, 'I'll order another bottle. Pay-day yesterday, you see. And you need a bit of a pick-me-up.'

Pick-me-up! thought Mrs Krane bitterly, holding her breath in dread. Now, if not before, she would come to grief.

She heard Katinka, her voice thick and altered but not without control, say, 'For God's sake don't make matters any worse than they are.'

So she must have seen Stordal and Jørgen go past. She could very easily have done so. The window of the parlour looks out that way. And she has some breeding, in spite of everything.

But what can you expect of an individual like Bowler Hat?

'Are they friends of yours out there?' he asked. 'Relations? In a little place like this everyone knows each other, I expect. Everyone except me, people like me. But they don't have to know who's in here. I want to see you look happy before you go home.'

'Happy? Go home? All I want to do is get away from it all. Shut the door, do you hear me?'

Katinka still had some sense, fair's fair. But you don't get anywhere with a drunkard who's got some fixation in his head. No breeding there, either.

'Just you keep quiet,' he said, opening the door a little farther and – heaven help Mrs Krane! – sticking his head out. 'Another half-bottle here, Miss.'

Miss!

He stood waiting in the doorway. Helplessly Mrs Krane looked at Larsen and Sønstegård. They returned the look with hostility and malice. Stordal, Jørgen and all the wives stared, gaping, at Bowler Hat. Stordal and Jørgen also looked as if they were trying to remember something. Finally they all gaped in astonishment at each other. Talk about a situation!

Mrs Krane gestured despairingly with her knitting needle. It was prudent to let the man have his way. Sønstegård rose, sucking her tooth loudly. Mrs Krane was despicable.

Bowler Hat held on to the door and waited, chewing on his cigarette, like the ill-bred scoundrel he is. That eternal cigarette butt of his can vex you beyond words. Nobody said anything, except for Stordal and Jørgen who were muttering together quietly and indignantly. The colour rose to the roots of Mrs Krane's hair. Sønstegård arrived with the tray. Bowler Hat took it, closed the door and drew the portière across so that it squeaked.

'Saturday customers, I see, and ugly customers at that. You ought to be a bit more careful, Mrs Krane. Whatever sort of party have you got in there?'

Mrs Krane did not reply immediately. Perhaps she felt just at this point that Stordal could mind his own business.

Sønstegård, on the other hand, had her answer ready. 'You may well ask, Mr Stordal.'

The ladies had made up their minds to go. They got to their feet and buttoned up their coats silently, their mouths tight shut. Even Mrs Berg Junior looked reserved. She nodded curtly to Mrs Krane as they all trooped out through the revolving door, one by one.

Mrs Krane went over to Stordal. 'Saturday customers. And Mr Krane's not at home.'

Then little Larsen had to chime in, 'Imagine having to serve people like that! Now, when we had improved things so much. All the gentlemen in to lunch, the respectable ladies in the afternoon, in the evening—'

'The less respectable.' Sønstegård sucked her tooth so hard that it hissed.

'Are you quite crazy?' said Larsen.

'That wasn't at all a kind thing to say, Miss Sønstegård,' declared Stordal.

'They're all right individually, I don't mean they're not—'

'Miss Sønstegård's such a tease, Mr Stordal. She enjoys provoking Miss Larsen,' attempted Mrs Krane in mediation.

'There's not *that* kind of difference any more these days, surely?' continued Larsen, determined to be the one to put matters into their proper perspective.

'I thought I noticed a difference.' Oh dear, Sønstegård and her bitterness!

'Tut, tut, tut.' Mrs Krane's knitting needle began jerking wildly, as if she were conducting a passage *furioso*. If these two were going to quarrel on top of everything else it would be too much for her, she knew it. 'We can't turn anyone away who isn't obviously drunk or rowdy,' she explained to Stordal.

Wisest to give him some information, however much he owed.

'If there's no drunkenness and rowdiness now, there soon will be,' Sønstegård assured them.

'You can't do a thing as long as people behave themselves, not these days. Quite right, Mrs Krane,' said Stordal gallantly. He turned to Jørgen. 'What were we talking about? Oh yes, women and money.'

And the quarrel was averted. Larsen and Sønstegård already had their attention seemingly riveted on the napkins again.

'I feel sorry for her too,' mumbled Jørgen rapidly, and so

quietly that he was barely audible. He looked sullen and guarded, as if suddenly in complete disagreement with his father.

'She has a great deal to atone for. She's never been able to accept life like the rest of us.'

Stordal's voice was harsh again; he probably thought nobody was paying any attention. 'She has sinned against the laws of life,' he asserted emphatically.

'All right, all right,' said Jørgen tensely. He had obviously heard it all before.

'She'll have to learn. I can safely say I did my best. It was no easy task. That I had to give up in the end – well, you'll understand that better the older you get. But don't misunderstand me. Always be kind and polite. She is your mother, after all.'

'And she's so much in demand, too,' said Jørgen. He seemed incapable of understanding that everything had to be the way it was, and clearly wanted to change the subject.

'There are certain unhappy creatures . . .'

Stordal got no further. The revolving door spun vigorously, and in came a gentleman dressed in travelling clothes and carrying a suitcase. He took off his hat and looked about him, surprised and seemingly disoriented. It was none other than Justus Gjør. Mrs Krane recognized him almost at once, even though it was many years since she had seen him last. It had been before she decided she might as well accept Krane. She had served in her father's dye shop and saw the townsfolk mostly through the window.

Stordal half rose. 'I'll be damned, surely it isn't—'

'Good afternoon, Peder Stordal.'

Justus Gjør looked searchingly at the person he was addressing, as he had always done. He had the same beautiful, slender hands and was incredibly unaltered, still one of those ugly men with charm. One and all had been sweet on him; it was a well-known fact, whatever the reason

64

might be. God knows, it might be possible to be sweet on him even now.

'Are you staying in these parts?' said Stordal, with a little more reserve.

'Newspapermen go everywhere, as you know. We're doing an investigation into the fisheries. Maybe you've seen it? The responsibility for this part of the country fell to me. Knew it already of course, and had nothing against a trip north again. I'm going farther east with the next steamer. Going to cover the whole of the Finnmark coast. But naturally I wanted to come ashore here. Is this Jørgen?'

'Yes, it certainly is.'

Jørgen bowed indifferently.

'They're growing up. I don't suppose his sister was born when you left? And here we are still. But you've covered a lot of ground since those days, haven't you?'

'Quite a bit,' said Justus Gjør, as if his mind was on other things. 'So you have a daughter as well?'

'I have. Good-looking girl, though I say so myself.'

'Of course you should say so. One must be permitted to be proud of one's children.'

At that point Gjør seemed to wake up and take notice of Jørgen.

'Good heavens, boy. You don't remember me, do you?'

'No,' answered Jørgen uncompromisingly.

'Why don't you run along, Jørgen?' said Stordal. 'I suppose you've got homework to do and all that? Remember you? Was he as much as two years old then? Just about, perhaps. What will you have, Justus? I'm drinking coffee, as you see.'

'With pleasure, with pleasure,' answered Gjør inappositely and absent-mindedly. But he had been vague before; had been famous for it, in fact.

'Tall, handsome lad,' he said, watching Jørgen go. 'Time flies.'

'Time flies.'

Time flies, thought Mrs Krane mechanically. What a

blessing the boy's gone. Now it's Gjør. Wasn't he a close friend of the Stordals? Weren't there even people who had said . . . ? Though surely that must have been nonsense? But now he and Stordal are capable of sitting there till the cows come home. Everyone knows what happens when men start gossiping. What a business! All those dresses that'll never be finished, Mr Krane in Southfjord too . . . It makes my head spin.

Inside the parlour it was suspiciously quiet again. The portière had been drawn across, but not entirely; Mrs Krane could tell by the sound of the rings. The one that was most inclined to stick had refused to budge. It would seem odd if she listened. On the other hand, she was responsible for the whole establishment. Cautiously she moved, in order to get her head nearer the door. For a long time she could hear only mumbling. Gjør and Stordal were talking quite loudly too. And Stordal had switched on the radio, whatever might be implied by that. It was still playing soft music from Copenhagen: 'Tea for Two'.

Mrs Krane gave a start. Suddenly Bowler Hat said loudly and encouragingly, 'There, you see. That makes everything better on an unbearable day like this, when all you can feel is that you've had more than enough of everything. You're tired out, Katinka, you know.'

So Katinka was boozing again. Perhaps she'd have to be carried out. She was talking drivel, for she answered loudly and clearly, almost in a singing voice, 'My eyes feel like blind glass in my head. They always do nowadays. But I don't bother about the spring any more . . . There must be a lot of people here,' she added, as if waking up, or as though she had made an unexpected discovery.

'What if there are? We pay like the rest of them.'

That voice again. How can you describe a voice like that? Rather indiscreet. It showed how far things had gone with Katinka for her to be tolerating it from a complete stranger, a lout. But – supposing a decent man had come along once upon a time and had talked to oneself in a voice like that –

yes, indeed. Mrs Krane's thoughts sailed off for a moment on the old sea of dreams they had sailed on daily in the dyer's shop, to which customers seldom came.

But what did he now have the effrontery to say? It was shocking.

'I don't wonder you say that about the spring. Tell me, you must have been in love once?'

'In love?' exclaimed Katinka, drunk, and taken by surprise.

'Did he leave you?'

'Leave me? I was married to someone else, he was married to someone else. In *love*? Some people are so in love with love they never dare to fall into it. They're afraid it won't measure up to their dreams.'

Does one say such things to a stranger? To a man? Definitely not, in Mrs Krane's opinion. Most definitely not, if it were true. Most definitely not then. Katinka's voice had turned peculiar now as well. It rose and fell in a most improper way.

'So it was like that,' said Bowler Hat. 'You were mighty pretty when you were young, Katinka. You're still pretty, if only you could shake off your difficulties.'

No accounting for taste, thought Mrs Krane. Today Katinka looked quite deplorable, with her hat awry, a button missing from her jacket, her face old and slack.

She must have been aware of it herself, for she replied angrily, 'Don't say things like that to me.'

'I must say what I think.'

Then Katinka laughed. An astonishing little laugh, clear as a bell. Was it really Mrs Katinka Stordal who was sitting laughing like that?

'There, you see? That's how you should sound. You know, you and I are alike. We understand one another.'

'Everything's so comical,' said Katinka and laughed again. They laughed together. As if he had never been the slightest bit shocking and boorish.

Then the conversation became so quiet that it was useless to listen any more. Stordal suddenly raised his voice. Emphasizing his words as if he were trying to shout somebody down he said, 'Let me tell you that there's one person who's managing splendidly, and that's Elise. You know I've never had much respect for women. But I take my hat off to Elise. An efficient person, let me tell you. A good position in the bank, appreciated by her employer—'

'So Elise's doing well? I'm glad to hear it,' said Gjør warmly and with animation. His mind seemed to be elsewhere again.

'So you ought to be,' was Stordal's guarded response. 'And what about you? You went off and got married again?'

'Yes, I did.'

'And—?'

'It was okay. Couldn't have been better. I'm a widower now.'

'Oh, hell! I mean, I'm sorry to hear that. I didn't know – I certainly hadn't intended to drag up . . . Did it happen some time ago?'

'A few months. Well – and what about you?'

'I'm a free man. You heard perhaps. Well, I've skipped the legal part of it, to tell you the truth. But that can be arranged at any time, a good many years have passed by now. I have a slightly better hold on the children this way. It can't be denied that they were a problem. Katinka, with all her good qualities, is quite incapable of managing her own life, let alone others'. Well, I keep an eye on it all.'

Gjør was clearly not interested in Stordal's family relationships. 'What else is there? Any building going on here?' he asked.

'In these times – no.' Stordal sighed, with good reason. 'But it will come, it will come,' he added. 'I'm not one to hang my head. In fact I feel younger and more optimistic than on many previous occasions. As long as you build your life on a little – if I may put it this way – joy, then . . . And that's what I've done. I've found much joy during the past two years. Happiness. But there, we can talk about that another time. And the town has developed, of course; a good deal, really. We've got a pleasant place down here, for instance, somewhere to go. My competitor has seen to the alterations, but you know I'm not petty about things like that. Credit where credit is due. It's attractive. It's comfortable. Hot lunches, dancing in the evenings, a veritable breath of the big city. We come here a good deal, Elise and I . . .'

Stordal suddenly broke off, as if he had said more than he intended.

'Oh indeed? So Elise comes here too?'

'She isn't one to hang her head either, let me tell you.'

'She's certainly never hung her head.' Gjør gave a brief laugh. 'That's not the way she expresses herself,' he said. 'Well – and what about Katinka? I heard she'd set up in the dressmaking business?'

My God, thought Mrs Krane. And here we have to sit listening to this, knowing that . . .

She looked across at Larsen and Sønstegård to see if they had heard too. They had, they must have done, the tables were so close together.

'So you know about that?' Stordal shrugged his shoulders. 'Good heavens, she's set up in the dressmaking business all right. But it's not simply a question of getting yourself established. She *can* sew, no doubt about it. That's a kind of talent too. But, but, but . . . You'll find her rather altered, my dear Justus.'

'Really? How is that?'

There was a keen look in Gjør's eyes. Mrs Krane remembered that look of his, from the times when he used to stand talking outside the dyer's shop. 'In what respect?' he asked.

'In every respect,' said Stordal.

The revolving door spun. In came Elise Oyen with that

69

fellow Lydersen. It was the time of afternoon when many people looked in. If Mrs Krane had not cleared the parlour by this time, she was unlikely to manage it now unless its occupants were to leave of their own accord, in front of everybody. That would be a nice thing!

Sønstegård sucked her tooth noisily and triumphantly. Sønstegård really was unbearable. Mrs Krane had touched on the idea many a time; now she thought it through to the end. But a good worker, in all conscience, non-unionized, indispensable.

She forgot Sønstegård in watching Elise Oyen. What did that woman do to herself to keep that way? Nobody would know she was well on in her thirties, least of all at this moment. Not only was she neat, well-dressed, good-looking and with just the right amount of make-up as usual, there was something completely new about her, whatever that might be. She probably had facials? At the hairdresser's? I ought to do something like that. If only I were not so tied from morning till night, I really . . . Elise Oyen looked the same age as the young wives. But nervous. Terribly restless.

Lydersen, also smart and dressed for spring, propelled her in front of him. It was obvious that neither of them had expected to meet Stordal, let alone Gjør, who had once been Elise's husband. They paused for a moment on sight, as if confronting a brick wall, but recovered themselves quickly.

Dashing fellow, Lydersen. And that way of his with women. Dangerously self-confident.

Scraping of chairs, exclamations, questions. Stordal could be heard saying to Elise, 'And what about you?'

'Me? Headache. Had to run an errand for the boss; got to be back again shortly. May I introduce Mr Lydersen, pharmacist, Mr Gjør, editor? This *is* a surprise, Justus.'

Mrs Krane had suddenly discovered what was new about Elise Oyen. It was the fox fur, the beautiful Arctic fox she was wearing around her neck. Who would have thought blue fox could be so flattering to the skin?

Larsen could not take her eyes off Elise either. She had to nudge Sønstegård: 'She's wearing it!'

'What? Which?'

'The fox fur, I'm certain. The blue fox. The one from Berg and Fure's window. She hadn't got it when she went past just now. Three hundred and fifty *kroner*!'

'Yes, you're right!' whispered Sønstegård, awestruck. 'Good heavens, has something happened to Stordal? Has he got hold of some money, d'you think?'

'Poof, she earns it herself. She can buy herself whatever she likes.'

In the meanwhile Lydersen was active with the chairs. The party arranged itself around Stordal's table. Larsen approached to take their order. 'Coffee please, that's all,' said Elise. 'Coffee,' said Lydersen.

Elise was sitting on tenterhooks, looking round incessantly, powdering her nose, chattering away without waiting for answers, her thoughts elsewhere. Her mind was busy with something, making her preoccupied. 'I thought you were at a meeting, Mr Master-builder. About the new school. The committee's in session, I know that, the boss went there some time ago. But why are we sitting here? Why don't we go in there?'

'Occupied, my dear,' said Stordal, interrupting her. 'By a mysterious party, a good-for-nothing with – well, with a lady or ladies. We've only seen the good-for-nothing, you see, but there are several of them. There was even something familiar about one of the voices we heard, but I couldn't decide who it reminded me of. They ought to be careful about letting the standard drop here. As for the meeting' – Stordal drawled it out – 'I went up with the new drawings. They promised to take a look at them.'

'My God! *Look* at them! And what about you, Justus? Nothing but affluence? Travelling and enjoying life? It's a different kettle of fish from sitting up here editing *The Pole Star*, I bet.'

'You're on an assignment for your paper?' threw in Lydersen courteously.

'Yes, more or less.'

'Justus is a widower, Elise,' Stordal informed her.

'Oh! I'm sorry to hear that, Justus.'

'That's life,' said Justus drily.

It was then that Borghild Stordal arrived, at such a speed that the revolving door was left spinning behind her. She always does move abruptly. She hesitated in the middle of the room.

What a day! Mrs Krane would have remembered it as the worst she had ever lived through, had it not been for the next, which proved to be even worse. She rose to her feet behind the counter, her face flushed.

Everyone looked at Borghild: Stordal with obvious pride; Elise with a dislike she failed to master for a moment; Lydersen, in the way he looks at pretty girls, from top to toe, with narrowed eyes and an odd expression about the mouth; Gjør with friendly interest. Mrs Krane felt as if she were at the theatre, but attending a disturbing and embarrassing performance.

The girl is good-looking. Tall and good-looking, with something about her that's wild and at the same time shy. When she grows out of that strange, stubborn personality of hers one day, something will happen. She's nicely dressed too. It's just that everything seems to fit wrongly, on purpose.

She was out of breath, clearly from walking very fast, and greeted them absent-mindedly and not at all politely. But with that mother . . .

She blushed violently, and looked away from them all.

And then, if you please, *she* made for the parlour as well. She walked straight up to the sliding door. That unfortunate parlour. It would be better to close it once and for all.

Mrs Krane placed herself deprecatingly in front of the door. 'I'm afraid not, Miss Stordal.'

She received unexpected assistance from Stordal. 'Now then, Borghild, you're in a great hurry? It's occupied in there, my dear, and goodness knows what sort of people are inside. Come and sit down here with us. This is my daughter Borghild, Justus. She was scarcely thought of when you left us.'

'Oh, is that so?' said Gjør pleasantly. 'Won't you sit here, Miss Stordal?'

'No thanks.' And Borghild made as if to go again.

'But—?'

'It doesn't matter, Father.'

Stordal was on his feet. He and Borghild were standing together by the revolving door. Mrs Krane could not catch what they were saying, but Larsen and Sønstegård could hardy avoid it.

'Something must be the matter, the way you rushed in. And the way you behave . . . Remember you'll be a young lady soon.'

'Do you know where Mother is, Father?'

'I? No, how should I know? Isn't she at work – It's a busy time just now.'

Borghild looked around nervously. Mrs Krane counted stitches as if her life was at stake, mumbling with a knitting needle in her mouth. At the table a lively, though quiet, conversation was proceeding. At least, that's what it looked like. Larsen and Sønstegård folded napkins, and the radio went on playing soft music.

'Tell me what it is, my child. They're all busy with their own affairs.'

'I thought, maybe she was sitting here and had forgotten the time.'

'In the middle of the day? That would be too bad, when she's got so much to do. Masses of orders, so I'm told. It's out of the question that she should . . . She's probably with one of her customers.'

'She's not with any of the customers. Good-bye, Father.

'Out on an errand, then? To get cotton? Pins? I don't know much about it. And surely she could phone for that sort of thing?'

'Yes, of course.'

'She'd damn well better look after that business of hers,' said Stordal in sudden irritation. 'That's one thing the rest of us can't do for her. Is it long since she left?'

'She was out when I came home in the lunch break, and when I came back from school she was still out. I must go now, Father.'

'Now listen, you must be a bit firm with your mother, Borghild.'

Mrs Krane, who was unable to distinguish any words from where she was situated, saw Borghild turn away and get out her handkerchief. According to Larsen and Søn-stegård's subsequent report she said something like, 'Nobody knows where she is. The telephone never stops ringing. It rang four times in the short while I was home. Torsen is at her wit's end. Mrs Buck has been waiting for goodness knows how long. She should have had a fitting at one o'clock.'

Stordal's eyebrows shot far up into his forehead. 'Hm, sounds like a nice kettle of fish.'

'I'm *frightened*, Father.'

'Frightened? Yes indeed – if this goes on, heaven knows what it might lead to. But she'll damn well have to pull herself together. It gets more and more urgent. She's got herself into this mess with the dressmaking. It was going to be so splendid, heaven help us. She was going to support herself, and the two of you as well. She was going to work it up so that she wouldn't need another øre's support. We were going to be free, the lot of us. Thank you very much – it's not just a matter of establishing yourself, there are certain obligations. This nonsense of being artistic about it – all well and good – but when it's a matter of your daily bread—'

74

He was working himself up into such a rage that Borghild shushed him. 'They can't hear,' he replied crossly.

'That's what you think.'

'They're all busy, can't you see?'

'That's another thing I'm frightened about,' said Borghild, and she turned to go out through the revolving door. As if against her will she hesitated : 'If only I knew what we could have for dinner. Torsen's there and everything. She must eat, even if we don't.'

'After all, it's worked so far. In its peculiar way.' Stordal dug around in his waistcoat pocket, but didn't seem to find much there. 'You see what *I* have,' he said, poking about in some small change he was holding in the palm of his hand. 'Not much to write home about. The building trade in these times . . . I pay for all of you, to the hilt. With all due respect to your mother—'

'If only I had a piece of sausagemeat for Torsen. There's some cold potatoes in the larder.'

'Don't bother me with the details. What about the account book? You used to have an account at Iversen's.'

'We haven't an account any more.'

'How's that?'

'It's your fault as well. Not just Mother's.'

'*What?*'

'More people are coming!'

On the brink of tears Borghild suddenly slipped through the revolving door, ran round the corner and up the hill, past the window of the parlour. Supposing Katinka happened to be looking out! But she was probably looking at that dreadful fellow and nothing else.

Nobody came in, thank the Lord. Not at that point. A young couple, up from the country, were walking downhill towards the quay. They were probably the people Borghild had seen. Stordal shrugged his shoulders, went back and sat down again. What could he do? All this mess was not his fault, Mrs Krane had to admit that, even if something did seem to be wrong somewhere.

Elise Oyen did not look up at him when he sat down. She could very well have done so, such good friends as they were. She looked away, without even asking whether anything was the matter. Poor Stordal almost looked as if he had expected her to. Then he threw up his hands and began talking about other things.

'Well, we've improved, haven't we, Justus? Isn't this pleasant? If we want one, we can order a good meal. A good glass of wine too. Nothing to complain about where the view is concerned. Wolf Mountain in the background; in the foreground the quay, with all sorts of activity. Do you remember how the Grand used to be? Dark and facing the yard, and commercial travellers getting drunk and disgusting. We put up with it. One must have somewhere to go. But here . . . I think it's the view that appeals to *me* most.'

Encouraging to hear, that's for sure, if only from Stordal. But for the moment Mrs Krane had too many other considerations in her head.

Justus Gjør laughed a little. 'I wondered what new place this was. I was really only going to ask my way. Didn't know whether the hotel or anything else was still in the same place. And then I run into Elise and you.'

'Wait till you see it in the evening. You'll be staying for several days, won't you?'

'Possibly. But I doubt whether I'll have time for an evening here. I've quite a lot of writing to do.'

'Good heavens, Peder,' interrupted Elise. 'What's an evening here to Justus, who travels about and sees all kinds of places? How can you think he'd be interested in this?'

'As an old resident of the town,' explained Stordal.

'Nonsense.'

She was so abrupt and offhand that it really was quite embarrassing. Lydersen, who was one of her previous flames – and who knows how they hit it off now, for things didn't seem to be so hot with Stordal any more – Lydersen tried to smooth it over. He leant forward and said, 'You're constantly on the move, then, Mr Gjør?'

'Constantly is an exaggeration. But there's always a certain amount of it. I used to work here on *The Pole Star*. That was before your time. But that was why I was glad of the chance to come north again.'

'I see. This place doesn't lack advantages.'

An odd thing for Lydersen to say when you came to think about it. His tone of voice was a little strange. It was as if for one reason or another he didn't feel entirely friendly towards Gjør. After all, he had been divorced from Elise a long time ago. And yet – capricious as she is . . .

An amusing notion, a clue to follow, if there had not been so much else to preoccupy one at that moment. Mrs Krane was not feeling calm enough to tackle new problems. She pushed them aside.

Justus Gjør seemed to notice nothing. He had always been the type who was above all that sort of thing. Had it not been said that he was rather patronizing, one of those who consider themselves to be out of the ordinary, a cut above the rest?

But an angel passed overhead, as they say, after Lydersen's comment. Or a lieutenant was paying his debts. It was quite quiet for a moment. And since the voices were simultaneously raised inside the parlour, Mrs Krane, whose hearing had improved considerably in a short time, heard Katinka say, 'I've become so wicked. Nobody would believe how wicked I am. It's as if I were poisoned. I haven't a kind thought any more. It serves them right, I think. I wish I could find something worse to do to them.'

'No wonder,' said Bowler Hat.

'It's the only means of getting away from them,' drooled Katinka. 'You don't get away from them just by leaving. You have weak moments, when they get the upper hand again.

'Everything around me is so ugly,' she almost shouted. 'I want it to be beautiful. For once in my life, I want it to be beautiful.'

'Loud-mouthed company,' remarked Stordal. 'Who the

devil does that voice remind me of? Such a pity in this attractive place.'

That was aimed at Mrs Krane, but it slid off her. Through the low-voiced conversation that rose around the table she listened as if hypnotized for Bowler Hat: 'Yes, it's not very beautiful in my home either. All I can offer you is those daisies. We'll buy them on the way. And I'd like to offer you so much. But – wait a minute – I have a ship in a bottle. I've got beautiful shells from all sorts of places – large, brightly coloured ones. I remember them now. They're lying at the bottom of the sea-chest. Those useless kinds of things you haul around with you. If you like, I'll get them out.'

'Useless things are the most necessary of all,' babbled poor Katinka.

'I have sunshine, when the weather's like it is today.'

'Sunshine?' shouted Katinka.

'I like to believe so. By the wall facing the sea I have a bench. It's only a plank, but it gets nice and warm there. I have an accordion—'

'An accordion?' cried Katinka, as if it were a matter of a grand piano at least. 'Sunshine, fresh air!' she shouted.

'Fresh air around you on every side!'

'Who's to stop us? Anybody can have sunshine and fresh air, even the poor. Come on, let's go!'

Dear God, Krane's in Southfjord, dear God, You know that, don't let there be any scandal while he's away. I'm not good at dealing with that kind of thing, it's not in me, You made me that way. Dear God, dear God . . .

Mrs Krane is said to have admitted openly later on that this was what she thought at that point.

A low mumbling came from the parlour. It had become alarmingly quiet in there, as if presaging some fearful event. Someone took hold of the sliding door. Slowly it slid a little to one side, and remained there an instant as if reconsidering. She heard Katinka say, 'It's all right, we can go. I don't care about them.'

And her voice! High, defiant, scornful, quite unlike herself. Whatever may be said about her, she was never a shrew.

All the same, Stordal and Gjør both seemed to get wind of something. They were looking around, narrowing their eyes in an attempt to search their memories. Just as Stordal and Jørgen had done. Elise and Lydersen exchanged fleeting glances. Oh God, now it will happen . . .

'That's the stuff!' The door opened wider. Bowler Hat stuck his head out and called across the room, 'I'd like to pay now.'

It didn't sound as if he was asking for it. He seemed to be giving an order. He was flushed and a lock of hair fell over his forehead. It was clear to everyone what kind of an individual this was. They all stared at him.

Mrs Krane signalled desperately with her knitting needle, to indicate that the only thing to do was to let the fellow have his way. She also made signs to the effect that they must be kept inside, he and Katinka, until the coast was clear. She was past distinguishing her own gestures any longer, and waved her arms about wildly.

Sønstegård refused to understand any of them. She simply set off without looking to right or left. She would!

Somebody coughed. It must have been Stordal. What right had *he* to cough, running up bills all the time? All kinds of feelings suddenly made themselves felt in Mrs Krane, she admitted later, including anger. Anger at being prevented from doing as she liked in her own café.

Doing as she liked. And what was that? She didn't know. She stood behind the counter making herself as scarce as possible, like children and animals when they're afraid. It doesn't help much; you can be seen just as easily. If Katinka and Bowler Hat were to leave now, right under the noses of the others, anything might be said in town. Trafficking, they might say. That dreadful word for what went on out at Rivermouth.

Presumably that was where they were going. Where does

a fellow like that live, if not there? He was not putting out to sea, not now at any rate, and not in front of their very eyes.

There was Sønstegård coming out again. And she was holding her nose demonstratively! Oh God, let it be just Sønstegård's antics, don't let them be sick in there! It was written all over her that she repudiated all responsibility. The way she was carrying her tray proclaimed it from afar.

The door opened wide, shooting back into the wall with a thunderous clatter. Out came Katinka, Mrs Katinka Stordal, mother of two lovely children, as Mrs Breien so rightly said. And she simply walked past the assembled company as if she hadn't even seen them.

After her came Bowler Hat, mockingly peering about him, chewing his cigarette and with his hat on his head. Katinka, on the other hand, was carrying hers.

She left without looking round, her head held high, as if in triumphal procession. The last they heard of her was that unaccustomed, bell-like little laugh. The revolving door spun a couple of times.

'Aha!' exclaimed Lydersen.

Otherwise nobody said a word for a long time. Then Larsen remarked, 'Well, I never did, in all my life!'

Mrs Krane burst into tears, openly, without attempting to hide herself. She snuffled and blew her nose; Sønstegård could suck her tooth as much as she liked.

Almost blinded with tears Mrs Krane caught a glimpse of Stordal. He sat looking as if he had just dropped from the moon. And why not? After all, Katinka had been his wife once upon a time, and she was the children's mother.

Lydersen gave a long-drawn-out whistle. Leaning forward, with his elbows resting on his knees and his hands lightly clasped, he looked attentively from the one to the other.

'Be quiet!' said Elise Oyen angrily. 'There's nothing to whistle about. There's no need to cry, Mrs Krane. It could have been worse. I'm the only lady present. And I don't take my dresses there. You do look thunderstruck, Mr Master-builder.'

Mrs Krane gestured away from herself despairingly with a sodden handkerchief. She was incapable of explanations, and incapable of controlling her feelings. But she wasn't crying only for the reason Elise had suggested.

And how should one explain Elise's behaviour? She was angry with Stordal too, even though he had not uttered a sound and was innocent of the whole affair. For surely he was innocent? Wasn't she suddenly standing there scolding him for something completely different? And making him look utterly shattered?

'The building could have been yours by now if you hadn't been so obstinate about that pergola. They don't want a pergola. Not in these times.'

'I've scrapped the pergola. I've given in on that point. For your sake, Elise, so that we might at last be able to—'

'Oh hush! A pergola! Overgrown with creeper! Here, where we have only two months of summer! And they're holiday months.'

'Yes, yes, yes. An attempt to include an element of beauty, a little romanticism, if you like. It would have been enjoyed by the whole town, considering the position of the new school. I've given up the idea, as I told you. My latest proposal is to build the gymnasium in one with the rest of it.'

Stordal's eyes were flickering helplessly as if he really didn't understand a word of what was being said. Lydersen's, on the other hand, were still, directed unwaveringly at Stordal.

'Bleken will get the contract, not you. People want everything functional nowadays, not old-fashioned aesthetics. If only you could give up those ideas of yours, Stordal.'

'I have given them up. That's exactly what I have done.'

'Yes, since Bleken got everything that's going. He builds this, that and the other, while you redesign the whole town in your imagination to look the same as it was a hundred years ago.'

'Pergolas aren't old-fashioned. In Hollywood—'

'Hollywood!'

'Congratulations on your new fur,' said Stordal, suddenly sulky and poised to attack. Not surprising either. Why should Elise bring all this up in the middle of everything?

'Thank you.'

'Couldn't you have waited a couple of days at any rate? You know it would have given me great pleasure. I shall get the advance payment on the doctor's glass veranda any day now.'

Poor fellow, thought Sønstegård. *Poor* fellow!

'It cost three hundred and fifty, my dear Peder.'

'Oh, damnation!' said Stordal.

'Well – a good fur . . .'

'Pure luxury.'

'Luxury? It's more of a necessity than you realize.'

'I'm sure there's a great deal I don't realize.'

'Oh yes.' Elise took out her powder compact and made improvements to her face. 'I'm telling you now, if it turns out that you have to take the children—'

'Now, Elise. Good Lord, things have turned out all right before, and they'll turn out all right again. There was a time when you talked about taking them.'

'For more than two years you've been saying things will turn out all right. It will turn out that not a soul will take their dresses to her establishment any more, not after this, don't you understand? Nobody will risk it. God knows they've been kind, but one day they'll get sick of having to fetch their dress material home again. I know what you're going to say: that she's gifted, and that's a kind of talent too. But when she refuses to make use of it . . .' And bless me if Elise Oyen didn't add quietly and terribly fast, but clear enough for those with sharp ears, 'You mustn't count on me this time. You must see to your own affairs, and you're two months in arrears. God knows, I'm not going to be responsible for your children going to secondary school and being the best dressed in town – and going to dances here at night. Or for Borghild taking tuition with Mrs Moe. Tuition! As if she were going on the stage. When I was her age I was out at work. *Take* them? My dear, I didn't know what I was talking about.'

'You were the one who wanted to bring them here. They needed a bit of fun, you said.'

'I thought so *then*.'

'But now they don't need it any more?'

'It's getting the upper hand. And when we see that their mother does nothing and behaves like this? Good grief, Peder, I can't take an interest everlastingly in those children of yours. I'll tell you one thing, Borghild is by no means as innocent as . . .'

Lydersen had begun twiddling his thumbs. He looked strangely expectant. Mrs Krane did not like his expression. What was it he reminded her of? Something lying in wait for its prey? A cannibal? Ugh!

'Borghild? She's like any other girl these days, isn't she? They're not the same as we were. As for her mother, things *are* going to turn out all right, she *is* going to mend her ways. So should I, did you say? Surely it oughtn't to matter what *I* do, as long as she sees to her dressmaking? . . . I can't understand why she hasn't learnt her lesson,' said Stordal, again looking as if he couldn't quite grasp matters. 'The simple fact that the rest of us enjoy ourselves down here in the evenings . . . she must feel—?'

'Oh God, you're naïve, Peder.'

'I'm naïve now as well? You're excelling yourself today, Elise.'

'Indeed?'

'What's the matter with you? I suppose you like buying expensive furs with your own money?'

'Yes, yes, of course. For heaven's sake shut up about the blessed fur. It's as if I'd bought I don't know what. It's not an expensive fur. It's just an ordinary, good fur.'

Mrs Krane's tears had dried completely during this exchange. Tensely, scarcely drawing breath, she followed this unexpectedly frank bickering. How could they forget themselves so, Stordal and Elise Oyen? At times they spoke quietly, but nobody else was talking. And at times they raised their voices quite high.

It was strange to watch Gjør too. With his back to the others, turned towards the window where Katinka and Bowler Hat had last been visible on their way up the street, he was staring grimly in front of him. But his cheeks seemed to twitch every so often, beneath each ear. He was rocking his foot backwards and forwards from heel to toe. He was not feeling kindly disposed.

But who was *he* angry with? It ought to have been Mrs Katinka. But it looked as if he was angry with everyone else.

He put his weight firmly on both feet. Stordal and Elise had stopped quarrelling; they were not looking at each other any more. Lydersen cleared his throat, as if expecting Elise to turn to him. She did not do so. As she was putting on her gloves she watched Gjør, who was taking Stordal aside into a corner. She was biting her lips as if wishing something undone.

Larsen popped up at her side. 'I think we can take it that spring has come,' she chattered, wiping a table unnecessarily. She refrained from referring to what had happened. One must be tactful. But that fur . . .

'The evenings are cold,' answered Elise incuriously into thin air, failing to notice what a splendid lead she had given Larsen.

'Yes, my word, one has to dress warmly. It's risky to go out at all at this time without something warm round one's neck.'

'Yes.' Elise's thoughts were elsewhere and she replied like

an automaton. Mechanically she fluffed up her fur, pulling at it so that the tail fell as it should, her eyes wandering towards the mirror.

Larsen could hold out no longer. 'What a lovely blue fox that is! So fashionable too.'

'Yes, it is nice.'

'I have a wolverine. It's a couple of years old, but it's not bad.'

'Oh, have you?'

Then Gjør broke in. 'Good-bye, Elise. Glad to see you're flourishing. Who are you going to catch with that fine fur, eh?'

Elise did not take it as a joke. 'You haven't changed, have you? Oh God, why did you have to turn up here?'

'Heavens, I'm leaving soon. But when Elise Oyen spends too much money, Elise Oyen has her sights on someone.'

'I haven't spent too much money. It was given to me. You're all quite crazy about this fur. An ordinary fur. Do I have to ask permission to wear a fur?

'My dear, of course not. So he's caught already?'

'Please yourself.'

'Are you really happy, Elise?'

'Yes, just imagine. Without politics, without social problems, without—'

'But with—?'

'Oh, get along with you.'

Gjør left, without another word to anybody, and disappeared into the street.

Lydersen had taken a little walk into the parlour. There he had been partly poking around, partly keeping an eye on Gjør and Elise. Larsen had been watching him the whole time; her eyes never left him as she listened and chattered. Larsen always watches Lydersen, so long as there isn't a wall between them.

She followed him in.

'What a ghastly stench,' remarked Lydersen. 'And what's that unattractive parcel?'

'It must be something they forgot.'

'If that kind of person's to be allowed to come and go as he pleases, this place will go downhill quickly. The parcel's warm!'

'Is it?' Larsen was wiping the table, although it was Sønstegård's and had just been wiped. She had to find something to do.

'Or lukewarm, rather. It feels as if it's a casserole or something of the sort, with a handle. Surely that's where the smell's coming from?'

'Well, it's nothing to do with me. It's not my table.'

Larsen suddenly felt affronted. Fancy going on about that parcel and acting as if nothing was the matter, now that they were alone for a moment! Was he going to pretend that nothing had happened at all?

'Damned if it doesn't smell of mutton stew and cabbage! They've forgotten their dinner. This gets better and better.'

'Does it?'

'Well, well, well, little Miss Larsen, mutton stew or no mutton stew, put me down for one coffee, three cakes, and a glass of port, will you? I'll be in again this evening. Oh yes, there was Mrs Oyen too – one coffee.'

'I daren't do it,' announced Larsen sourly. 'Mrs Krane won't have all these bills mounting up. All of you want everything put down.'

'You're not afraid of Mrs Krane.'

Lydersen looked round, made a quick decision, and kissed Larsen behind the ear.

'No!' whispered Larsen, about to faint.

'Yes.'

He kissed her once more, and went. Just outside the door he almost ran into Sønstegård. She *might* have seen. The probability was that she *had* seen.

'Did you get wind of something again, old lady?' he

hissed. 'I can't stand your prying ways. If you think you're going to profit by it . . .'

Sønstegård sucked her tooth. She was on her way in to her tables in the parlour, on an honest errand, and had nothing but contempt for vulgar insinuations.

Elise Oyen was leaving. She had already given the revolving door an initial push, but paused. Lydersen made straight for her. Just as it should be. She was his companion; he had arrived with her.

'Did you see your boss too? Just in time. Perhaps leaving here in the middle of office hours doesn't look too good.'

'Thank you, that's my affair.'

'All right. But we came here to have a little chat.'

'Fat lot of chat we had. But it's not necessary.'

'No? I'm delighted to hear it. Why are you so angry, then? You were in a good temper when we arrived.'

'Is it any of your business?'

'Don't get so excited, little Matilda, I'd have thought it was. To change the subject, there *is* something odd about you today, I've noticed it all along. What's the reason? It can't be just that splendid piece of fur?'

'How like you men! You can't see anything unless it's under your nose. Yes, of course it's the fur. Nothing besides the fur. I must go. Good-bye.'

Mrs Krane had manoeuvred herself closer, tidying over and under the counter.

Now Elise was bickering with Lydersen. What a quarrelsome mood she was in!

Bent down behind the counter, moving boxes of chocolates and other objects backwards and forwards, Mrs Krane heard Lydersen say, 'Tell me – was it a false alarm, perhaps?'

'Will you help me or won't you?'

'I can't run the risk of . . . And I did give you—'

'Are you such a fool as to run risks? And it didn't help. Nothing but dishwater. If I have to take Peder, it'll be your fault.'

'I'm on night duty tonight,' said Lydersen.

'Are you?'

'Come the back way. As you used to. Three sharp taps on the window.'

Elise did not reply.

Oh God, how Mrs Krane's back was aching. She had to straighten up for a second and managed to catch sight of Lydersen as he took Elise by the arm.

'Now, no nonsense. You're through with that old man. The other one's through with you. So I'm the only one left. You ought to be thankful. For that ex-husband of yours, who's just popped up, can't be counted on. Now we've had our chat after all.'

Still no reply.

'Nice fur,' said Lydersen. 'Really very nice.'

'Perhaps he's not through with me after all,' said Elise defiantly.

'His wife's coming on the next coastal steamer. A nice fur is quite appropriate. A very sensible investment.'

'You're a cad.'

'Yes, thank God. You don't get far by being respectable.'

Mrs Krane had manoeuvred herself along to the other end of the counter, and popped up behind it, stiff and sore from her crouched position. She watched Elise leave and then noticed Stordal, who was still sitting lost in thought on a chair by the wall, and had clearly not yet collected his wits. 'Elise!' he called, as if waking up. But she was through the door already. It revolved many times behind her, she was so furious.

Mrs Krane managed to sit down dazedly in her place behind the till. She was sore in her back and in her soul. There was Larsen. What was she carrying?

'This parcel, Mrs Krane, may I put it in the kitchen? It ought to have been taken away long ago, it smells so.

Imagine leaving something like this! It's something they forgot. It seems to be mutton stew.'

'Take it out,' said Mrs Krane, weak with exhaustion.

Larsen, too, looked exhausted. But she had the strength for a gibe at Sønstegård.

It hit the mark. Sønstegård was not without weapons. She was a tough customer; she herself called it being hardy. She looked up for a moment from the table-napkins and said, 'What a face, Miss Larsen! Nothing has happened to you, I hope?'

'I should mind my own business if I were you. Here I am, having to clear up after you.'

'A good thing you don't bite.'

Stordal at last got up to go. He actually seemed older in his walk and appearance than when he arrived. The poor fellow. And Elise Oyen was so mean to him, on top of everything else.

He paused in the middle of the room and raised his head. Suddenly he had that stony expression on his face that can make you feel quite scared. 'There are people who will never learn from life, who continually batten on the rest of us. It will go badly for them in the end. And without any doubt it's right and proper that it should go badly for them. But it's depressing to witness.'

He continued towards the door. His little speech had bucked him up considerably, he was quite himself again. When he put his hat on inside the door he placed it way over the back of his neck.

'Quite right too,' said Sønstegård. 'Good Lord, are you crying again, Mrs Krane? What's there to cry about? What's done is done. No use crying over spilt milk.'

'If we always knew what we were crying for . . .' Mrs Krane wept more profusely than ever.

'If only we knew how this scandal was going to end.' Sønstegård gave the knife in Mrs Krane's anguished heart a final twist. 'But someone's coming. You must pull yourself together.'

And somebody did come. It was the young couple up from the country who had passed by a while ago, and who had finally plucked up courage and entered the splendid café.

Two complete outsiders. With completely innocent faces.

SCENE TWO

The following day the weather was abominable; snow flurries and storm, as if it had never been spring. It was a Sunday too, and Sundays are quiet. Both facts were used by Mrs Krane to excuse herself – as if they had anything to do with the matter.

She got her punishment. And it was well deserved. But you had to pity her, poor thing, pity such stupidity and helplessness.

The café opens at one o'clock, after morning service is over. As a rule scarcely anybody turns up before evening. There's a bit of coming and going, fetching of cakes and so on, but that's all. People are out walking or skiing, depending on the time of year. After church they go back home with their friends for a glass of wine. In filthy weather they stay indoors, as on this Sunday. Not a soul to be seen in the streets.

Unless it happens to be a national holiday, of course.

Sunday is the most boring day of the week at the café. Even so, it can be pleasant sometimes to sit in a place with central heating. Quite a few people seemed to think so that Sunday, at any rate.

You think Bowler Hat's place must be damp and uncomfortable? Did he and Mrs Katinka deserve anything better? Doesn't it serve people like that jolly well right? To sit stuffing yourself at Krane's with the whole town agog – that's a real treat. Mrs Breien is supposed to have knocked on the door several times, far out at Rivermouth, and been given their lip on each occasion. Buck is supposed to have gone there and threatened them with the police. They only laughed at that; at any rate Bowler Hat did, for nobody managed to get a glimpse of Mrs Katinka. He merely stuck his nose out to deliver insults, and then slammed the door again.

Gjør is supposed to have been there. The door was not even opened to him.

Yet they arrived, wet and bedraggled, but not in the least ashamed or embarrassed. On the contrary, head-in-air. They marched into the parlour as if nothing were amiss and placed a sizable order : sandwiches, cakes, coffee. To crown it all Bowler Hat went across and felt the radiator, to see if the temperature was satisfactory. What cheek! He had hung his clothes over it to dry, too. Sønstegård noticed that the last time she took in their order.

Naturally both she and Larsen took for granted the idea of fetching someone – Buck, Mrs Breien, Olsen, the Police – when they noticed Mrs Krane standing there spinelessly without saying a word. Sønstegård had thought at first of refusing to serve them, but then it occurred to her that they were a fine catch. Best to hold on to them until the appropriate authorities arrived.

And then Mrs Krane didn't even suggest hurrying to fetch this person or that She positioned herself by the sliding door, knitting for dear life and listening. Ridiculous. What was there to listen to? Was the old woman curious as to what two drunkards sat drivelling about? Perhaps it would be wise to put a telephone call through to Krane, since his wife didn't have any better sense? The future of the café was at stake.

Surely that was no exaggeration?

Sønstegård sucked her tooth as loudly, disapprovingly and frequently as she was capable. Neither she nor Larsen said a word, as they sat over their paper napkins. They coughed now and again, tight-lipped. They were cross, and with good reason.

The snow flurries beat against the window-pane and the storm shook the house. But then, it was April. The grey sky hung low; it would get dark early. Out of doors not even a cat was to be seen.

Through the loudspeaker came Listz's 'Nocturne', played by Moritz Rosenthal, but softly. Why didn't Larsen turn it up a little? Ask me another.

Mrs Krane talked a great deal of nonsense afterwards. The worst was probably all that gaggle about there being something so strange about the fellow's voice, you would have nothing against it if anyone talked to you like that. Not a good-for-nothing like him, of course – and yet . . . Who then, Mr Krane? No, he wasn't that sort. She meant it really as an excuse for poor Mrs Katinka, since she's too foolish not to have given up that kind of thing, at her age.

Mrs Krane is pretty foolish herself.

She was certainly not happy, standing there full of contrition for all that she dimly felt she ought and ought not to do : contrition for demeaning herself to listen; contrition because there was something about the very impudence of the man in there, about his hair falling over his forehead yesterday and his flushed face, that made her wish she had experienced it herself – something that was not respectable, Mrs Krane knew it all too well.

She stood there on that dreadful Sunday, which was going to be far worse than she could ever have dreamt, and heard, with fear and trembling, the voice say : 'Let's have half a bottle of wine with this, shall we?'

It would take courage to ask Sønstegård to serve *that*. To go herself – that too would take courage.

'I daren't,' answered Katinka. Mrs Krane breathed a little more easily.

'Daren't? Who's to stop you? Let's have half a bottle at least. You need a pick-me-up. Damn it all, we could have had some music, if it weren't for those creatures outside. We could have left the door open, if you weren't so scared, poor dear. The radio's playing, but it's on low. Music makes you happy.'

'Happy?' And then Katinka said something that did make you feel sorry for her, even though she had brought the whole thing on herself: 'They sang after me. They sang after me again.'

'What if they did? They sing after a lot of poor devils. They don't understand misfortune. Or sorrow. They're too stupid. Stupidity is worse than spite. The public is always on the side of the lucky ones, you must have noticed that. If only I had a better place to live in we'd never have come here. But when rain and snow pour in, what can one do? I was afraid you'd come to harm. If it weren't a Sunday . . . Tomorrow I'll get hold of some planks and tiles. I've been lazy about it. I'm an old sea-dog and a bit of wet doesn't hurt me.'

'We should have gone somewhere else.'

'You thought those boys who did the singing would follow you there. They might have done too. And nobody comes *here* on a day like this. People who're in the habit of coming here are sitting at home digesting their dinners. Meat balls and – apple pie and all that – roast beef and rice pudding and liver paste. That's all good stuff, isn't it? What about liver paste? Do you like that?'

'I don't know . . .'

'But this evening we'll be the ones to build up a big fire again. And then we'll get out the accordion. The last song I played last night – you liked that one, didn't you? How many times did you ask me to play it? Four? I know music always makes you happy, as long as you dare to be happy . . .

'Just don't give a damn,' he said more loudly. 'Let them bloody well sing! What harm does it do you? Let them all go to the devil! Let them sit there yattering in their Sunday best.'

'Do you think my children have heard them sing? Do

you think they sing within earshot of the children as well?'

'Good Lord no. And supposing they did? The children despise you as it is. Don't give a damn about them either – any more than they give a damn about you. They're slave-drivers, like all the others.'

'But then they can suddenly be so kind – '

'When they want something, yes. And then you're finished straight away, remember.'

'They know so much about all kinds of things and so little about life. Sometimes they can look quite bewildered.'

'Yes, and as hard and spiteful as the devil when they think there's something to be had. And they think that all the time. But you mustn't be unhappy. We'll hit on something. You're going to get rid of this misery.'

'I should have done so yesterday, when I almost had the courage.'

'There, you see. Now then, we're going to have that half-bottle . . . Miss!'

Mrs Krane got away only just in time, the door was thrown aside so violently. In her confusion she pretended to be on her way back from somewhere to her usual post. And yet he smiled scornfully, the dreadful fellow.

'Half a bottle of port, here. And biscuits. Quick as you can, please.'

The ladies simply looked at each other, and no one made a move to get up.

'Oh, Miss Sønstegård?' said Mrs Krane at last.

What a coward! Instead of showing both of them the door; instead of fetching the proper authorities. Krane's café had to give shelter to those sort of people, bolster them up, pamper them, while respectable folk had the wool pulled over their eyes. Sønstegård sucked her tooth with particular ardour and conviction, as she slowly rose to do Mrs Krane's bidding. She almost pulled a face.

Bowler Hat waited in the doorway as usual, took the tray and closed the door behind him so forcefully that it was a wonder nothing flew to pieces, that the door frame didn't crack. That would have been something for Krane to come home to. What behaviour!

Sønstegård remarked on it too. 'Good thing the house didn't fall down,' she said.

But Mrs Krane simply looked puzzled, as if she had noticed nothing.

There she was at the door again. She could do *that*. But let her stand there. Let her be the one to decide when to call in the authorities to carry them out.

'They're pouring it out . . . they're drinking it . . . they're pouring it out again,' mumbled Mrs Krane as if in a trance.

'Fancy that! Did you hear that, Miss Sønstegård? They're *drinking* the wine they ordered!'

Larsen's tongue could be sharp as well. She looked up, proud of herself: 'Yes, of course I heard. No end to the strange things that go on in this world.' A pithy comment that made Larsen bubble over with laughter. Sønstegård was old and far from good-looking, certainly well over forty, thin as a post, and she could be a bore. But her head was screwed on in the right place, that you had to admit. Had Mrs Krane heard her?

It didn't look like it. Paralyzed with dismay Mrs Krane was listening to Katinka. Katinka was drunk again. 'A-a-h,' she sighed, and then laughed. And although everyone knows she's never been farther south than Trondheim, she explained, 'After all, I've been on a long voyage too.'

'Tell me about it.'

'It was monotonous. A grey sea without end. Each day came towards you like a heavy, enormous breaker. As soon as you woke up you could see it coming. It swept over you, swept over the whole ship, you understand, it blinded you. There was mist too, you could never see farther than the next wave. For a short while I managed to jump ashore on to a rock, but—'

'But?'

'No, that was all. I slipped down from the rock again . . . Or it disappeared. I don't know, I don't know . . .'

And suddenly Katinka almost shouted, loudly and excitedly, 'But now I don't give a damn about it all. Why should I go on here and . . . ? Why on earth? Let me roll in the gutter, let me stagger about drunk, let me make a pig of myself. It's my affair, isn't it?'

Shameless, thought Mrs Krane, thoroughly shocked. And shameless of them not to have drawn the portière across. They're no longer afraid of anything. That I should have let them in! That I can never learn! I, like the rest of them!

But Bowler Hat was saying, as calmly as if Katinka had been talking about the most ordinary things, 'You mustn't give a damn about people. They get cocky if you do. And if you want to find out who your friends are, be poor. Then they trickle away, one by one. If any of them remain – well, they may be all right individually, but in general they'll make use of you to suit themselves. You need someone to help you against that lot. But there – until you found yourself on that ocean – how was it then?'

'Still. Clear weather. *Too* still. *Too* clear.'

'That's how it is, to begin with. And now? Shallows and reefs and fog? Difficult to hold course?'

'Course? There is no course. I don't seem to exist any more, I'm right under, head and all. All I think about is money and food. At my age—'

'At your age? You're young enough, and pretty into the bargain. I think you're pretty. Besides, plenty of people aren't so particular. They've learnt to be more concerned with someone's character . . . Have you really never travelled?'

'I was in Trondheim once, to learn dressmaking. At Matheson's, the best firm in North Norway. I was already separated then. It was during the war, people were earning money, I was able to borrow a little. It was fun as long as it lasted. We sewed beautiful things there. Really beautiful.

It was chock-full of lovely materials. If you had any spare time you could go and look at them and make them up in your mind's eye. They said I was good at it. But then I came back here. And here . . .'

Katinka, who had been talking quietly and reasonably enough for a while, suddenly turned crude again. 'I was married early, you see. That's what happens to us here, we take the first one that comes along. What else are we to do? Some of us have illegitimate children, but most of us get married too . . . *Skål* !'

Her voice was grating and strange.

'*Skål.*'

'Have you ever felt how it can hurt to handle things? When you get that tiredness in the palm of your hand? When simply having to touch something is repulsive?'

'When you're fed up with everything, you mean? And wish it all to hell?'

'Something of the sort, yes. Everything's ugly.' And Katinka started shouting again, as if to a deaf man, 'I can't bear all this ugliness any more! Ugliness and untidiness! Scraps and pins everywhere. And washing-up! Oh, that washing-up!'

'The dishes? Oh yes, of course, they leave the dishes to you, to say nothing of the other chores. I can just imagine it. But now it's you who're leaving them, and for good.'

'For good?'

Mrs Krane twisted and turned with anxiety. Good gracious, what were they thinking of? Then the voice began again, and she was drawn helplessly along with it, 'I'd do the dishes for you and a good deal else, as long as you'd stay with me. I can darn and cook, most seamen can. What would you like to do? What would you like to potter about with all day? What would a woman like you have to do to be really happy? It's a damned nuisance being poor. But if only you'd come and save me from my loneliness, I'd always hit on something.'

And now it was he who raised his voice. 'Loneliness is

hell. Loneliness is the cause of everything that's low and filthy. I won't be lonely any more! D'you hear?

'Forgive me,' he added, and his voice was pleasant again, you might almost call it – yes, my goodness, you would have to call it tender. Surprisingly clear as well, in spite of its being so quiet; quiet and piercing at the same time. 'Forgive me. But no one can hold out if they have to live as I do now. We must be made for something else? Don't you think so?'

But talking to a drunkard is like talking to a brick wall. Drunkards can talk at cross purposes endlessly. Katinka went on with her own preoccupations.

'Do you know what it means to go round with words on the tip of your tongue? Low words, dirty words, that make you feel degraded simply for thinking them? They lie ready inside you just the same. Like – like embryos. Wanting to get out. Oh God, there are so many of us living like this. We swarm over the whole earth.'

She had reached the stage of being earnest and full of confidences. Mrs Krane knew all the stages; she had seen plenty of that before the alterations. It was the morning after as well, with all that that entails. Naturally they had been drinking at Rivermouth last night, on top of what they had put away here. They were still recharging themselves.

'The best thing is to come out with those very words,' stated Bowler Hat adroitly. 'They can't be so foul that others haven't deserved to hear them. No, they're certainly not as foul as all that.'

'I want to get away from myself. I don't want to be spiteful and wicked, to use vulgar weapons that make me squalid.'

'Your weapons? And what about other people's? You won't leave any dangerous wounds, you may be quite sure. Poor you. No – but look, how beautiful. A blue vein and so very white around it. White, white, white.'

'Let go of my wrist!'

'Old age will come one day. Real old age. You'll be lonely and unable to work. Poor. Do you think they'll bother about you then, those children of yours?'

Katinka did not reply to this, so far as Mrs Krane could tell. But how strange to be moved by the things he *said* as well. It wasn't only the voice.

'Someone else ought to have a chance of looking after you. Someone else . . . If only he were allowed.'

Silence again. Sønstegård sucked her tooth so that it whistled. Larsen coughed. They were sitting over there nursing their own opinions. Was it their café? Were they anything more than employees here? Nevertheless, they themselves probably wanted to listen in.

'I have a bit put by,' said the voice again. 'I'm not as poor as all that. Can you sing?'

'Sing? I could sing once. That was a long time ago.'

'Then you still can. As long as you're happy again. Listen . . . we could travel, you and I. We could go round the farms playing. I play well enough on the accordion, you heard that. We could be free. I'd become a different person if I had a sweet little woman to live with.'

'I'm old, do you hear?'

'Nonsense, you're still young. Young enough. And I look for character, as I told you.'

'You're kind.'

'Kind? Rubbish. I'm clinging to you. We need each other. But you won't stay. I have a feeling that you won't stay. No one will stay with somebody like me. It's as if I had the plague.'

'Don't talk like that.'

At that moment the revolving door whirled violently, and in came Mrs Breien, red in the face from wind and snow flurries, her hair tousled, her clothes soaked. She put down a dripping umbrella that immediately made a large puddle around itself. If Sønstegård and Larsen had not been annoyed with Mrs Krane, one or other of them would have got up and gone to fetch a floor-cloth. Now, neither of them made a move.

'Is Mrs Stordal here?'

Mrs Krane had hastily manoeuvred herself away from the door. She too was red in the face. 'To tell you the truth, Mrs Breien—'

'I don't see why you shouldn't tell me the truth, on top of everything else. You're letting her sit here boozing two days in a row. Is she in the parlour?'

'If it were up to me . . . Mr Krane's in Southfjord. It's not easy for *me* to refuse to serve people. And in such terrible weather.'

'It is up to you. You're acting irresponsibly. As for the weather, Mrs Stordal has a home of her own. She *still* has one. She has it today. Nobody knows what she'll have to-morrow – she and her children. If all three find themselves on the street, you won't be blameless, Mrs Krane. I wouldn't like to be in your shoes when that happens.' With which Mrs Breien pushed the sliding door firmly aside and went in. It was easy enough to hear what she was saying.

'You must be ill, Katinka. Seriously ill.'

'Ill?' Mrs Stordal laughed defiantly. 'Poor people aren't allowed to be ill, surely you know that. You say to poor people, "It'll pass, you'll see. Don't worry. Now let's pull ourselves together, shall we?" That's what you say to poor people who are ill. Surely you know that, Constance.'

'Rubbish! You're talking rubbish. Either you're out of your mind, or you want to change the subject. Psycho-paths are supposed to try to talk other people round, you know. And I mean the *mentally* ill.'

'You're always so full of horrifying stories, Constance. I suppose you think I'll learn from them, and admit that I'm really perfectly all right. But things aren't improved one iota by the knowledge that other people suffer too.'

'What are you babbling about? I've never heard any-thing like it.'

'I'm not babbling. I'm talking honestly for once, talking about things as they are.'

'I've had to tell you a few home truths now and then, give you examples. I suppose that's what you're referring to. Certain truths that were not very pleasant to listen to, such as the matter of having a little foresight, planning a bit. Yes, I'm thinking of time as well as money. Some people are born with that ability, others are not. It's not easy to acquire it, but it's possible, and I think I know what I'm talking about. It has simply been my duty to mention it. But we don't want to talk about that now. I've come to fetch you, Katinka. I've come out in this weather, on your account, to get you back home and indoors. With your children. All I want is what's best for you – you know that. Come along now.'

'I'm not going home. Because I've held out before, you think I can go on holding out. You're mistaken, I can't. Life has no consideration – I have no consideration, not any more. We're quits.'

'What empty talk! I've heard you harp on about that before. It always happens when you're not quite yourself. My poor Katinka.'

'Harp on about it? I'll twang the strings so that they grate on your ears.'

Here that blasted Bowler Hat interfered, the impertinent lout. It didn't improve matters.

'That's the stuff,' he said. 'Let them have it right on the kisser. Don't complain. If you do they'll come clinging to you with their pity. And I'm telling you, pity kills. They'll use it to suck the marrow out of you, like leeches. They can make mincemeat of a person. Don't let them get their teeth into you, d'you hear? They relish it so. They get such a kick out of it. They're so kind, you see. But you'll be finished, you can bet your life on that. What do you want to answer them for, anyway? Hell, don't answer them, it's none of their business. Don't let them creep up on you with their endless chatter. Stand up for yourself!

Not a word now, whatever happens.'

Like the lady she is, Mrs Breien had treated Bowler Hat as if he were thin air as long as she could. Now she could contain herself no longer. She exclaimed, 'What a frightful person you are! A real devil! Is it clear to you that that's what you are?'

'It's clear to me that you're a bloody bitch. A proper baboon. Get out!'

'I could report you to the police for saying that.'

'And I could report you for calling me a devil – if it amused me. It doesn't amuse me.'

'If you stay here after this, Katinka, you have indeed sunk low.'

Mrs Breien's voice was full of well-bred patience. She was above indulging in any further repartee with Bowler Hat.

Katinka followed his advice. She made no reply. A glass was put down roughly on a plate in there, either hers or his. Then somebody laughed, a high-pitched, uncontrollable laugh. It was Katinka, who else could it be?

So Mrs Breien left. With a sigh she collected her dripping umbrella and said good-bye to nobody in particular. She considered the establishment as a whole to be guilty, there was no doubt about that. She dragged herself clumsily through the revolving door and was gone.

Mrs Krane sank on to her chair, speechless. She had got herself into a thorough mess, heaven help her.

From inside the parlour they heard, between two bursts of laughter, 'She means well, you know.'

'She likes playing Providence. A bloody old bag like that, poking her nose into everything. *Means* well? What good has she ever done you? Has she ever done anything for you besides make you so disgusted with everything you could throw up? You say nothing? Just as I expected. But I know the type. My mother-in-law's exactly the same. I can hear her now: "All I want is what's best for you, dear Nissy". My name's Nils, you see. Run around the place spouting twaddle, that's what they do, these old cows, while some poor fellow sits somewhere slaving away for them. D'you remember she said yesterday that her husband was nervous? He can thank her for that. Does *she* ever do an honest day's work? Does *she* sew? Does *she* wash the dishes? I enjoy seeing you laugh, but what's so funny about it?'

'Everything. Your calling her an old cow.'

'She is an old cow, a half-baked old cow into the bargain.'

'She's a clever housekeeper, you know. Ha, ha, ha!'

'My mother-in-law is too. Damned efficient. Women of my class *can* work all right. But this one? Damn me if she has the time for anything more than flouncing about making others miserable . . . *Skål*! Ha, ha, ha!'

'*Skål*,' said Katinka in a deep, husky voice.

'Drunken riff-raff,' said Sønstegård loudly.

The sliding door was closed, rapidly and with a thud.

'Oh, my Lord!'

It was Larsen who first caught sight of Borghild Stordal, and by that time it was too late. Borghild was almost through the revolving door. She was soaked, without a hat, without an umbrella. Her hair was plastered about her face. She looked neither to right nor left, but went straight into the parlour, opening the door an inch, squeezing in and closing it behind her. At once Mrs Krane, Larsen and Sønstegård were all at the door, with their ears against it.

It really was their duty. Just in case anything happened.

They heard Katinka break off in the middle of a peal of laughter.

They heard Bowler Hat: 'Look who's here! The young madam. I'd know who she was anywhere,' he continued severely. 'Lord, that's obvious. But hell, surely we're human too? Are we through with being human because we've brought that lot into the world? . . . Good-looking girl,' he said more calmly. 'Mighty good-looking. So that's what you used to be like.'

He spoke in that voice against which Mrs Krane had no resistance.

'Your bed's not made,' said Borghild.

'Make it then, if it displeases you. And go away. You've no business here.'

'That's how to treat them,' said Bowler Hat. 'That was good.'

'They're coming to fetch their dresses tomorrow. Nearly everyone has phoned to say so.'

'The dresses are theirs.'

'We've had food sent us – ready cooked. Anonymously, as if we were poor people.'

'Aren't we poor people? We were given food yesterday as well. What happened to it, by the way? It was for you. Too bad I should have lost it.'

'Torsen's come to work today as well. She's trying to get something ready, at least.'

'Poor Torsen. Doesn't she understand that it's no use any more? It's too late. Those dresses will never be ready. You must explain that to her, Borghild.'

'Do you simply loathe us, Mother?'

And just imagine, Katinka Stordal answered, 'Yes, I loathe you. You whip me through life like an animal.'

'We do?'

'You too.'

'So now we know,' said Borghild bitterly.

'So now you know.'

Imagine saying something like that to one of your children! Katinka couldn't have been simply drunk; she must have been mad.

Borghild suddenly exploded. 'Imagine growing up like you! I'm not going to be like any of you. I'm going to be different.'

Whatever did she mean by that? She must have been referring to her parents. She couldn't very well have meant

Katinka and Bowler Hat. How could he come under consideration?

'You must go now, Borghild. It's no use staying here, talking. I'm not listening. One day a great numbness descends. That's your salvation. Then everybody can save their breath.'

'We thought we were your children.'

'I thought so too. One thinks so much. I had hopes and wishes for you both, I wanted all sorts of things for you. And then you turn out to be nothing more than strangers, demanding and expecting one thing after another – "We'll squeeze it out of her. That's what she's for." And afterwards you remember only the time when I couldn't manage it, when you couldn't squeeze any more out of me. You're like all the others – pulling and pushing, pulling and pushing.'

'But Mother—'

'You're not to stay here any longer, Borghild.'

And all of a sudden Katinka shouted at the top of her voice, 'Here comes the madness, the great, wonderful madness. The liberator from everything, who opens the gates and makes all spacious about you.'

She laughed wildly; hysterically perhaps one should say. At any rate, it was the most horrible laughter Mrs Krane had ever heard. She put her hands over her ears, staggered away, and sat down in her chair behind the counter.

'Surely we ought to fetch somebody now?' said Sønstegård.

But Borghild was rushing out. She looked at nobody, simply disappeared through the revolving door.

'Perhaps she's going to fetch someone,' sniffed Mrs Krane, deluged in tears once more.

'It's all very well to cry,' said Sønstegård scornfully. 'Why not do something?'

Somebody was crying in the parlour too, violently and convulsively. They could hear so clearly because the sliding door had been left ajar by Borghild, she had drawn it behind in such haste. Softly – in *that* voice – Bowler Hat tried to comfort her: 'No wonder, when they've been so unkind. You just cry, it helps sometimes.'

And Katinka did cry. After a while she sobbed, 'I haven't the strength to fight them.'

'Hm, if you can't do that you're lost. Then you might just as well gather your traps and go.'

'They cut one to the quick, over and over again. I've been cut to the quick long enough. I'm not in duty bound to do more. No . . . break out of it all, cover my tracks after me . . .'

'Christ, that's the stuff. If those people always get their own way . . .'

And the door slid to with a bang.

'This can't go on, Mrs Krane,' announced Sønstegård.

The revolving door swivelled around. It was Borghild again. And Gjør, pushing her in front of him. She was reluctant, but he was holding her by the arm. The snow was lying thickly on the brim of his hat and at once began trickling down him, back and front. He had turned up the collar of his raincoat.

Mrs Krane breathed more easily. It was Gjør, Justus Gjør; probably the best person to arrive at this moment.

'Here you are, Miss Stordal,' he said to Borghild. 'Sit down here. Yes, come on, sit down. You're going to have something warm, and then we'll talk.'

Since Borghild still refused, he forced her into the chair and began to unbutton her overcoat. Only when he had got it off did he throw his sodden hat on to a peg and take off his own coat.

Borghild sat looking numb and lost. She did not even greet Larsen when she approached them.

'Tea for two, if you please, Miss. Good, hot and strong, with plenty of boiling water. What can we have to eat? Can you make us some toast?'

'I should think so.'

'And butter and marmalade. Or – perhaps you'd like a proper meal, Miss Stordal? I'm sure we can have something. Fried eggs and ham, what would you say to that? Isn't that right, Miss, you could make us that?'

'I should think so. We don't serve hot lunches on Sundays, but—'

'Thank you, just tea. That would be nice,' said Borghild. She sat pushing her wet hair away from her face, her teeth chattering loud enough to be heard. And bless me if Gjør didn't bend down to feel her shoes, just as if she were a baby. Larsen waited for a moment to see if Borghild was going to change her mind about the tea, so she saw him do it with her own eyes.

'Take off your shoes,' he ordered. 'We'll put them on the radiator to dry. Pull down your stockings, so that the wet part is away from your feet, and sit with your legs drawn up under you. Nobody'll come here in this weather, and we'll try to avoid a bad cold. Won't you have a little brandy before your tea?'

'No thank you.'

Borghild kicked off her shoes obediently, looked a little embarrassed when Gjør felt her stockinged feet as well, but otherwise took it all quite calmly. Borghild, who's supposed to be so modest! Borghild, who made for the door on one occasion, red as a lobster, in the middle of a dance with Lydersen. There he had stood with open arms, looked about him and said, 'Blow me if I understand the girl!'

'Thank you, I'm all right now,' she said, and drew her legs back under the chair.

As she was leaving, Larsen heard Gjør say, 'How did you manage to get so wet? Did you *forget* your galoshes? You mustn't do that, you know. Not in weather like this.'

No indeed, we must hope nobody will come, thought Larsen, with such extraordinary goings-on, outside as well as inside the parlour, the likes of which have never been seen at a respectable place before. The mother drunk with a common fellow in the one room, the daughter almost bare-legged in the other, with – not a common fellow exactly, but a complete stranger. Not even from the town. It would have been fun to hear what they were talking about.

According to subsequent reports from Mrs Krane and Sønstegård there was a long silence at first: not a word was exchanged for some time. Gjør went across and turned the radio up higher. It had ceased playing Liszt's 'Nocturne' long ago and had been giving a mumbling lecture that nobody had noticed. It embarked on the waltz from *Harlequin's Millions*. A lovely waltz, that's for sure. All the same, Mrs Krane and Sønstegård would rather have done without it just then. They caught a sentence here and there, quite a few too, when the conversation got going. It was about Katinka, but went slowly to begin with. Borghild was looking about her uneasily, and Gjør spoke very quietly.

'. . . a radical change is necessary, and at once,' he said a little more loudly, lighting a pipe and puffing at it.

They were silent again. Then Borghild said, 'We could have gone in there, if it weren't for—'

'We could have gone up to my room at the hotel. Only it's so damned uncomfortable there, and – well, I'd rather bring you here. You know what small towns are like. It was closer too, and you needed to get indoors.'

Borghild blushed again. As if there was nothing else to blush about. There was a pause.

'. . . if only she'd go to bed at night and work during the day. And wouldn't sit messing about with dresses for me, on top of everything else. I tell her, "Don't bother, Mother, I don't care what I look like". That's not the sort of thing I care about.'

'What do you care about then, Borghild?'

'Oh . . . I don't know. There's a lady here who used to be in the theatre. She's married now, with masses of children

too. But she teaches, you see. I go and read with her along-
side my school work. Poetry and bits of plays and that sort
of thing. I suppose it's stupid, but—'

'I don't doubt it's very wise.'

'Now I suppose I'll have to finish with that and going
to school. I'd have liked to take my matric too.'

'You're not going to finish with anything. That's the
sort of step that only makes matters worse.'

'Yes, but . . .'

The conversation came to a halt again; at least that's
what it looked like. But when the waltz was over, and was
followed by an endless station signal, Sønstegård heard
something strange.

'I'm not afraid of you,' said Borghild.

She looked embarrassed as she said it, and well she
might. Fancy saying something so childish!

But Gjør took her quite seriously. He looked at her
searchingly. 'I hope you're not. It would be a pity if you
were. Are you afraid of anyone else, since you—?'

'I'm afraid of almost everybody. And if I'm not afraid
of them, I think they're boring.'

'Oh, indeed. So I'm one of the boring ones?'

'You needn't talk to me as if I were baby.'

'That wasn't my intention at all. On the contrary, I –
I'd very much like to talk to you as an adult, Borghild.
There's nothing I'd like better at this moment.'

'Do you mean that?'

'Yes, I mean it.'

There was another pause, then a muted conversation, impossible to catch. Borghild sat looking down at her lap.
Then she must have forgotten herself, for she talked quite
loudly again. Her teeth were still chattering, so that she
spoke jerkily. Peculiar things she said too. Looked as if
the daughter would be as mad as her mother soon.

'Take me with you down south . . . let me come with
you.'

Justus Gjør removed the pipe from his mouth and

busied himself with it thoroughly for a while, scraping it and knocking it out. For some time he said nothing. A concerned furrow drew his brows together. 'I thought you said you wanted your matric?' he asked.

'I shan't get it anyway. Not now.'

Silence again.

'I'd work very hard,' said Borghild breathlessly, as if she must talk fast once she had got going. 'I'd work at anything . . . I'm nearly through with junior high now . . . in a couple of months—'

'Better to put that couple of months behind you first,' said Gjør. 'You must take your matric as well.'

'Must? You're only saying that to get out of it. It's not better to put something behind you, not better to hang around here for three years to get your matric. I'm in a hurry – a terrible hurry.'

Gjør was leaning his elbows on the table, puffing at his pipe and watching her. 'I understand you have a great deal to put up with, Borghild, and it's difficult for you. But for the moment there isn't anywhere you're needed as much as you are here. A great deal depends on you. Your mother is very fond of you, and—'

'Fond of me? Only a short while ago she said that—'

'Oh. You knew a long time ago that what we say in this life and what we feel are two entirely different things. And surely there's not all *that* hurry?'

'For me there is.'

'Who are you afraid of, Borghild?'

'I told you, lots of people. I told you, almost everybody.'

'But these people are very ordinary on the whole. They're not in the least remarkable, and certainly nothing to be afraid of. One day you'll laugh because you let yourself be impressed by them. Of course, you lack any comparisons in small towns, it's true.'

'I'm not impressed by them. I know they're not so great. I . . . I look down on them. That's why . . . why . . . I'm afraid of myself most of all.'

She seemed to let the last sentence burst out in spite of herself.

'That's another matter,' said Gjør.

Larsen arrived with the tea. There was a clinking of cups, and so many repetitions of 'Drink it while it's hot', and 'Won't you have this, Miss Stordal?' and suchlike, that the conversation lost interest. The radio plugged away at another waltz, a lovely waltz. It was even called 'Illusion'.

When the noise quietened down again, Sønstegård heard Borghild say, 'I wonder how far they get? Whether they do get very far?'

'Who?'

'The ones who leave.'

'The ones who leave?'

'Yes. In modern plays they always leave in the end. I'm going now, they say. I've often wondered how they managed after they left. They can't live up north, at any rate they don't have to take the coastal steamer. You have to have at least seventy-five *kroner* to do that. And for that you'd only get as far as Trondheim.'

'I expect you're right, Borghild, they probably don't live up north. It would be a bit thoughtless of the writer, at any rate, if he let them do so.'

'Now you're making fun of me. But if you're a boy you can sign on with a ship.'

'That's true. I suppose plenty of people have done that.'

'Yes, plenty. A girl has to walk the length of the coast instead.'

'Rather a long walk.'

'Now you're making fun of me again. You're the kind who likes teasing. But I'm not afraid of you.'

'I'm glad about that, Borghild. I'm glad you're not afraid of me. I feel honoured.'

'Well then, don't make fun of me. For I don't suppose anything will come of it? Of going south with you, I mean.'

'I'm afraid it won't. I—'

'No, I expect you're right.'

'Your chance will come.'

'My chance? I'll go to the dogs – that's what my chance will be.'

'Borghild, how can you say such a thing?'

'To the dogs. Here one goes to the dogs.'

'Not you. You'll go out into the world. You'll be clever . . . and happy . . . and beautiful. Very beautiful, Borghild.'

'Me, beautiful? I look a fright. It's only because there's something nasty about me that they're—'

'That they're—? What were you going to say?'

'That they're after me?'

'*After* you? Who's after you, if I may ask?'

Sønstegård could not believe her ears. Borghild Stordal – that young girl – sitting there saying the most incredible things. After her? Yes, one in particular, and Sønstegård knew who that was. Borghild was sought after when there was a dance at the café, it couldn't be denied. But sullen and obstinate as she was, nobody got much further with her. She was only a child anyway. And deep down she obviously liked being popular just as much as the others. But she had to pretend, to be different from everyone else. When it came down to it, she was not above asking Gjør to take her south with him. Because otherwise she would go to the dogs! What a lot of excitable rubbish! Nobody goes to the dogs unless they have a mind to. And then that nonsense about not being attractive! She knew very well that she was. But there are all sorts of ways of making yourself interesting. Ugh, there was Larsen scraping her chair as she sat down. Couldn't she try to be a bit quieter? But she was cross because she had forgotten the hot water, and had had to go out again to fetch it.

Sønstegård sucked her tooth.

But Larsen, who did not know what the matter was, craned her neck and said, 'He's standing at the kiosk.'

'Who?'

'Lydersen of course. Isn't it the Polar Bear* that's open today?'

'Is he coming here?'

'Heaven knows. Yes, maybe. Yes, I think he is.'

Larsen patted her shingled hair absent-mindedly.

'Fancy going out in this weather! And when he ought to be on duty.'

'It's spring now, you know.'

'Go on with you, you and your spring. Is it spring today? Looks as if he's waiting for someone.'

'He's looking in this direction.'

'Expect he's looking for you.'

'Or you.'

'Or . . . ?'

Sønstegård knew the art of pin-pricking Larsen's heart. At the same time she made it known by her gestures and expression that there were more important matters than Lydersen to take note of at the moment. Borghild's voice, which had been quite quiet for a while, was raised again :

'We're just a burden to her.'

'It may seem so.'

'It *is* so.'

'You know at heart that's not really true.'

Sønstegård and Larsen were once more in full sympathy. They chatted on, seemingly about the weather, but they pricked up their ears. For moments whole statements went by the board; for moments they emerged and threw light on their surroundings.

'Everything's as bad as it could be since we've been without regular help for the dressmaking. Now we turn night into day all the time.'

'Unhappy people often do that.'

'But it only makes everything worse. And even now, when there's such an awful lot of work, I find her making things for me. Things for me to wear when I get my

* Chemists' shops have such names in Norway, e.g. The Pole Star, The Swan.

114

school certificate. A dress and a suit and underwear and . . .
I tell her, "You're crazy, Mother, bothering with all this
now". Then she goes on about wanting me to look
pretty.'

'And you still doubt that she's fond of you?'

'No, I suppose not. And the way it looks at home. Pins
and scraps of material all over the floor. She used to pick
it all up every evening. Now she says it doesn't matter,
she's got to sit up late at night sewing in any case. It's
enough to send you crazy, all those half-finished dresses
hanging over the backs of the chairs. And the telephone.
But it's all over now. They'll all take her work away.'

'Now, listen to me, Borghild, you and I must put our
heads together . . .'

The revolving door spun around. In came Lydersen, wet
and bedraggled. He looked round with a dissatisfied expression. Clearly he had not expected this exactly, though
it was difficult to guess whom he was looking for. But he
was polite enough. 'Good afternoon, Mr Editor. Filthy
weather. And there's Miss Stordal. Good afternoon. No, I
won't disturb you, I'll sit over here. Thought of having a
look at yesterday's papers over a cup of coffee. You'll
excuse me, won't you?'

'To be sure,' said Gjør indifferently. He was watching
Larsen and Sønstegård, who hurried across to Lydersen's
table, both talking at once in high good humour. 'Gracious
me, are you out today too? Aren't you on duty today,
then? The Polar Bear's supposed to be open today, isn't
it? And in this weather!'

'Absence makes the heart grow fonder.'

Lydersen unfolded a newspaper, looking at the clock
and then at Borghild who, clearly embarrassed, was attempting to get into her wet shoes and pull her stockings
up properly. She turned away, scarlet and trembling, while
tidying herself up.

Gjør was busy with his pipe. Again it needed to be knocked out and filled. But he was a strange man. He seemed to miss nothing, that was Mrs Krane's impression. She almost made up her mind to talk to Gjør as soon as Borghild was out of the way; get him to make Katinka see reason.

'Do you *close* on Sunday afternoon, then?' flirted Larsen, whose table Lydersen was sitting at. She wiped it over and over again, patting her hair repeatedly.

'We ought to. People could keep off aspirin and castor oil one afternoon a week. Do 'em good. But you forget, girls, that we have a chemist at our establishment, an exceedingly kind chemist, who sometimes comes down and relieves his poor assistant. We have an apprentice as well, a first-class apprentice.'

Lydersen was talking for the sake of talking, no doubt about that. Sheer balderdash. If you're on duty, you're on duty, and that's all there is to it. That was obvious even to Larsen's simple brain. He was watching Borghild, who had put on her coat and was taking leave of Gjør.

'I hope I'm not chasing you away, Miss Stordal?'

The question was left hanging in the air. Gjør said, 'Hurry home, get those wet things off your feet and get started on what we agreed about.'

He too picked up a newspaper, an old one into the bargain, turned over the pages as if looking for something special, and disappeared behind it.

Borghild hurried out. Lydersen turned to watch her go. He raised his eyebrows as if something quite peculiar and extraordinary had happened. Then he asked, 'Tell me, isn't the parlour free today either? The door's closed, I see.'

'Oh, it's that fellow again,' exclaimed Sønstegård.

Mrs Krane looked at her threateningly. Surely she needn't have said that? Was she an employee here or wasn't she?

'But good heavens, this really won't do, you know. Are

you going to put up with that type of person from now on? Daily, so to speak?'

And he asked, by raising his eyebrows and tossing his head, whether the fellow had company today as well? The same, perhaps?

Sønstegård nodded and sucked her tooth.

'Scandal,' said Lydersen. 'No other word for it.'

'He is quite revolting,' said Larsen.

'Regular customer here now, is he? He and his lady friend?'

But Lydersen isn't exactly suited to playing the role of the man of principle. He's a marvellous dancer, it's true, he livens things up in the evening and brings in the female customers to a certain extent. For this he's given a good deal of rope in the matter of signing chits. But that was as far as it was going.

Mrs Krane remarked a little stiffly, 'The man works here on the quay, he's been here a couple of times. You can't turn people away in weather like this. Not people who pay for what they get.'

It's an advantage to have a quick tongue. Lydersen got what he deserved. But if he looked at a loss, it was only for an instant. And Larsen, who arrived unexpectly with coffee and Danish pastry, mixed herself up in it in her thoughtless way.

'He's been here at night, what's more. Came in just as he always does, hands in his trouser pockets and his hat on. Anything as impolite as that fellow! The place was crowded, as you might expect. I suppose Mr Krane thought it would be embarrassing to say anything – after all, people up from the country and suchlike come here. But he was relieved when the fellow went, I could see. It's not that the man works on the quay, that's not what I mean—'

'No, of course not. But ill-bred. Unpleasant appearance.'

'Ugh, yes. Those eyes. He seems to be looking straight through you.'

Lydersen was bored with the topic, however. He went on chatting nervously about the first thing that came into his head.

'Is that so, little Miss Larsen, does he look right through you? Clever of him. Now then, don't be cross with me. It's attractive to be a bit, you know,' he said, gesticulating feminine curves. 'Too much slimness bores me.'

Suddenly seized with uneasiness he looked across at Sønstegård. Sure enough, she was sucking her tooth and clearing her throat into the bargain.

'Of course, it depends on the type,' added Lydersen, hastening to modify his last comment. 'What suits one person doesn't suit another. Some people look better thin. But to get back to this fellow, there are decent cafés down at Rivermouth, in the alleys there. Someone ought to suggest to him that he goes there. Country folk are quite different.'

He took out his watch.

'Four,' Larsen told him.

'Thank you very much.'

But Larsen had something else on her mind, a great deal on her mind. 'It's beginning to be lovely in the evenings down Strand Street now,' she suggested.

'Ugh, I'm thankful to be indoors,' said Lydersen shuddering, at once on his guard.

'Yes, when it's like today. But when it isn't like today, I mean. Like yesterday, for instance.'

'Get along with you,' said Sønstegård, nudging her. 'Have you begun courting already, Miss Larsen? Isn't it a bit early? A bit wet on the roads?'

'Oh, as long as you're with someone you like, it doesn't matter. Besides, there must be places where you can shelter—'

'Yes, the summer cottages,' snorted Sønstegård. 'If you're the kind that goes into the cottages.'

'What nonsense you talk, girls.' Lydersen looked at the clock again. 'I must go. Write it down for me, won't you,

Miss Larsen? End of the month, you know.' He said it
lightly, throwing on his raincoat and hat. 'Mrs Krane . . .
Mr Editor—'

And he was gone as if spirited away. The revolving door
spun.

Mrs Krane got to her feet. She must pull herself together;
she must talk to Gjør. She had been sitting preparing herself for a good while.

At that precise moment he put down his newspaper and
came over to her. 'It's true, isn't it, that Mrs Stordal's in
there? In the next room?'

'Yes, I'm afraid so, Mr Gjør. Oh dear, Mr Gjor, if you
could . . . So that nothing really dreadful happens, I mean.
Her children are quite big, and—'

'If I'm not disturbing Mrs Stordal I'd very much like
to have a few words with her,' answered Gjør, without
any reference to the situation. He certainly was superior;
he could make you feel like a stupid child.

He knocked on the door.

'What the hell is it now?' came the reply from inside.

'Excuse me.' Gjør quietly slid the door back, just enough
to allow his tall, slim figure to pass through. 'I do apologize.' And he pulled it to behind him.

Mrs Krane was there at once, and Larsen and Sønstegård. They put their ears against it. Why pretend any
longer?

They could hear Gjør.

'Well, here you are, Katinka. I've been running around
looking for you all yesterday and today. I didn't want to
leave without seeing you, I'm sure you understand that.
Then I heard you were in here. I hope you won't mind my
interrupting you – under the circumstances— I'm here
for only a short time . . .'

'Yes, I was out at your place too,' he said to Bowler Hat.

'A good many people have been out at my place.'

'The door was shut. I don't think you were at home.'

'I may very well have been at home. I open the door when I feel like it. If not, I don't.'

'Quite right too.'

'Oh, you think so, do you?'

For a while nobody said anything, nothing that could be heard outside, at any rate. Then Gjør said, 'Do you remember me, Katinka?'

'You're Justus,' replied Mrs Stordal, but in such a quiet, tired voice that she sounded quite strange.

'Won't you let me walk home with you? So that we can have a chat? As we used to do. I should tell you that I'm an old friend of Mrs Stordal's, passing through town.'

The last remark must have been addressed to Bowler Hat again. As if he was worth bothering about.

'No, not home,' said Katinka. 'It looks so dreadful at home. And now, when I've been away too – away for a while.'

'I'm not the sort to bother about that. You know I don't notice such things.'

'But I notice them. Pins all over the floor, you see. I can't be bothered to pick them up. And scraps of material. Ugly and horrible. Come back tomorrow, will you, Justus? I have company now, as you see.'

'And what a place this is,' said Justus. 'All of you seem to spend your time here. It looks as if none of you could stay home any more.'

'It's a place to go to, you know. A bit of a change.'

'It's a pigsty. It smells of decay – stale tobacco and spilt wine.'

Mrs Krane looked at the others indignantly to see if they had heard. And yes indeed, they had heard. How unjust, how hare-brained! This attractive place. But it was all Bowler Hat's fault. It was because he was sitting there, giving the wrong impression. Do her good to get such a slap in the face. But she was thinking: No help in Gjør, if that's how he is.

'I don't understand you,' said Katinka. 'We think it's a pleasant place.'

Her voice was the same : tired, quiet, worried, patient.

'I don't know when I'll get my orders to leave, Katinka. It may be tomorrow, it may be the day after. And it's ages since I last saw you.'

'There's no steamer before Wednesday.'

'No, no, that's possible. But I have a good deal to do as well.

Silence.

'Is this the one you were in love with?' said Bowler Hat brazenly and tactlessly.

'You can't stay sitting here,' said Gjør, ignoring him.

'She'll stay here as long as she likes. D'you think she cares for you, or for any of the rest of them? What the hell are you all making such a fuss about? As if she were a child or a lunatic?'

'Leave me alone, Justus.'

'Leave her alone.'

'I only want what's best for you, Katinka. Nothing except what's best for you. You know that.'

'You're kind, Justus. I remember that. Fancy your being up here again ! How nice. Sit down and have a drink. No – that's true – not now. Another time.'

'Another time? When I may have to take the first steamer going south or east?'

'You come and you go. It's no problem for you.'

'I've been here since yesterday. I've met Peder, I've met your children. Now I'd like to meet you. But perhaps it's stupid of me to want to?'

'No, it's very nice of you, dear Justus.'

'Oh, to hell with it ! How *are* you, Katinka? How are you managing? When I heard that the two of you had separated, I thought now she's got her freedom – to act, to be herself—'

'Freedom, yes. To stand outside in the bitter wind. To freeze. A woman alone . . . How am I? It gets better towards evening. I've another day behind me. As long as I have something to put me to sleep. Without that . . .'

And suddenly Katinka switched to that drunkard's voice, full of twaddle and confidences : 'We're created for warmth, Justus. We're created to be loved by someone. Imagine, I've discovered that. If we were not like that the world would stand still, we take so much on our shoulders when we . . . I'm telling you, Justus, we take on a great deal.'

'Now let me take you home.'

'No. Not home. I won't go home. I want another drink. I've been invited to, don't you see? Without it being in the least unpleasant! Imagine that, Justus!'

'Quite right,' exclaimed Bowler Hat.

'You don't know what you're saying. You're rebelling against everything. And it's not surprising, as far as I can judge. But you mustn't get mixed up in anything that'll make it worse.'

'That was aimed at me, of course.'

'It was not aimed at you personally. I'm sure you understand that. But Mrs Stordal has let everything slide, making greater and greater difficulties for herself and her children. There must be a change, a great change. But this way's no good.'

Justus Gjør was talking to Bowler Hat just as if Bowler Hat were an old friend and he was in the habit of discussing such matters with him. He was a queer fish too, that Gjør, if not a half-wit.

'Yes, those children,' said Bowler Hat angrily. 'Bullies in need of a good hiding, like all kids.'

But Katinka was banging on the table with a matchbox : 'Hey there, more wine!'

They took no notice of her. Even Bowler Hat said nothing. He must have realized it was no use any longer. Yet Gjør said, 'Is this you, Katinka?'

'This is me. At last, this is me.'

There was silence for a little while. Then Gjør said, 'I do recognize you all the same, I recognize the part of you that couldn't be cowed. I don't know what to call it. Something indomitable that wanted to go its own way, and could have become creative. It often made you impatient. I remember well that blue dress of yours that was so attractive – it was beautiful. Once, while you were making it you threw it into a corner and burst into tears. You couldn't get it right, you said.'

'Creative! That's good, Justus. Creative with your mouth full of pins, up to yours knees in material and thread. *Skål!* Oh dear, my glass is empty.'

'Creative people have to stand up to their knees in all kinds of things before they're through. But what you're doing now is simply stupid. It's your life that you're throwing into a corner now.'

'I don't give a damn.'

And Katinka began talking twaddle again, full of confidences: 'At times you actually get the idea that you *can*. Can what? Well, *can*. Right out of the blue, you know. It's as if you're on top of a wave. When you're down again – it couldn't be more bloody. I'm fond of sewing, too, if only it didn't make you tired. Beautiful materials that you can fashion as you like and put on a beautiful person, it's enough to make you dance for joy. Or sing. Stupid, did you say? That's stupidity. There are always so many of them, in such a hurry, and you can't see clearly any more. Your eyes feel like blind glass stuck in your head. Or someone comes – you should see them – absolutely shapeless, insisting on clothes like a young girl. They bring the material with them, utterly crazy, impossible material that can stand up by itself. They insist on having it made up as if for a seventeen-year-old with frills and gathers. I tell them they can have it this way and that, then perhaps I can make something out of it. But, oh no! Finally I say, "Go to someone else, here are the pieces!" I let them talk me into cutting it out, you see, they get me that far. I do try, it's my living, and I have the knack, as they say. And "Dear Mrs Stordal, you can do it in the twinkling of an eye you're so clever—" '

'But all that can be changed, Katinka.'

'It's obvious you've been away, Justus.'

'First of all we'll go home.'

'I won't go home. I told you, it's ugly at home.'

'Your daughter is at home, tidying up. I'm not entirely helpless either. We—'

'Oh, how naïve you are. I hadn't remembered you were naïve.'

Katinka's voice dropped threateningly. 'The time is ripe. You must admit it, all of you. *Ripe.*'

Silence.

Then Gjør said, 'Come over to the hotel with me, then. Just so that we can have a talk.'

'What have we to talk about?'

'Shouldn't we have something to talk about?'

'No.'

Precisely at that exciting moment Mrs Krane, Larsen and Sønstegård were given something new to think about. They had been standing there in the twilight that comes creeping up early on such a day, had heard far more than they could digest immediately, and now . . .

The first one to realize what was happening was Sønstegård. She was standing facing that way. It was some time before she could believe her own eyes. She went across and turned on the lights and had to believe them. There were faces behind the wet panes, pressed against them with their noses flattened. They disappeared, others took their place, in ones and twos, sometimes several at once, blinking in the light that had fallen on them so unexpectedly, grinning, disappearing, reappearing. The snowflakes and the flattened noses changed their shape, as a poor mirror does.

Sønstegård gripped Mrs Krane by the arm. 'Now there'll be a nice hullabaloo, won't there! Crowds of boys from

Rivermouth outside. All we want now is for them to decide to come in.'

'But they never come here. Not any more.'

A thoughtless remark on Mrs Krane's part. And much too easy for Sønstegård to answer, answer so that it stung, 'Not any more? My dear, this has turned into just the place for that sort of person. Rumours fly fast. You may be able to stop them looking in from outside, Mrs Krane, but you can't stop them coming in.'

'Ugh, how horrible,' shuddered Larsen. 'What a blessing that fellow Gjør's here. That's what *I* think.'

Voices could still be heard inside the parlour; its occupants did not seem to have noticed anything. Mrs Krane sat down behind the counter. In desperation she supported herself with her hands on her knees. She did not even reach for her knitting.

The revolving door circled repeatedly. Sixteen- and seventeen-year-old youths, of the kind who are capable of anything in gangs, streamed in. They shook the water off their caps, tossed them up on to the pegs, felt the radiator, gathered at different tables in what seemed to be different groups. But the understanding between them was obvious from the start.

A disturbing atmosphere filled the café. It was expressed in humming, in the exchange of cheeky, sly remarks, in tramping that gradually fell into a common rhythm, a rhythm familiar to the whole town. The humming followed the tramping like a buzz, rising and then falling suddenly again.

Mrs Krane got to her feet and stood trying to look authoritative. She barely succeeded, she was aware of that, not least because Sønstegård was sucking her tooth in triumph with a didn't-I-tell-you-so expression on her face, while Larsen stood dumbfounded as any little girl. There were too many of them to be turned away, especially with a man like Bowler Hat in the parlour, who might appear at any minute. Besides, there wasn't much to criticize as yet, beyond the fact that they were a bit rowdy and looked the way boys look when they're planning mischief. As long as they hadn't done any mischief, and as long as Mr Krane was in Southfjord . . .

Before she could collect herself they had begun giving their orders.

'Orange squash here, please.'

'Bottle of pop.'

'Milk for me.'

'Coffee.'

Larsen and Sønstegård were already flying here and there with trays. Boys were crowding round the counter choosing cakes. Mrs Krane scarcely had time to draw breath, as she carried out their orders, cake-server in hand. She could hear nothing from the parlour; she wasn't near enough, and it was too noisy in the café. Much too noisy.

The singing and tramping rose and fell, dying away momentarily, to rise energetically from another part of the room, then sink to a weak hum. Here and there a few individuals dared to throw out a few words as well. Mrs Krane recognized the song.

Waves of fever passed through her, her hands were damp and chilled. When the humming rose once more and threatened to break into open song, with a great effort she pulled herself together.

'Now then, that's a bit too lively, don't you think?'

Quiet for a short while. Through it Sønstegård's victorious tooth-sucking was audible. That sucking of Sønstegård's! Whether she approved or disapproved it was equally irritating. Especially when she disapproved, naturally. If she had a rotten molar she ought to do something about it.

'We're only singing a bit,' said someone.

'This isn't a concert hall,' said Mrs Krane as genially as she could.

'But it's a dance hall.'

'That's a different matter.'

'That's what you think.'

So she knew that the worst would happen. It would happen soon. She looked at the tables. Many of the bottles and plates were already empty.

'You shouldn't occupy so many tables for too long at a time,' she attempted, feeling quite giddy as she did so. 'Other customers may come at any minute. Then we shall need the room.'

'Oh, if anyone's coming today they'll have come already.'

Sønstegård's face! Mrs Krane knew she hated it.

At once, as if at a signal, one of the boys sang quite clearly, 'Hm-hm, hm-hm's sweet on me', and hummed the rest of it.

Sønstegård could not help giving a snicker. That was quite clear too, and encouraging without a doubt. Larsen did not fare any better, but she at least held her hand over her mouth, and looked guilty.

'We're not going to have any commotion here. We're not going to have any singing. Those who have finished must go.'

Mrs Krane was really severe that time, outwardly at any rate. Her heart was hammering.

'Another orange squash here.'

'One bottle of pop.'

'Another cream slice, please.'

At once Larsen and Sønstegård flew hither and thither. Ugh, they were like schoolgirls suddenly finding the courage to do something not really permitted.

> 'Hm-hm, hm-hm's sweet on me,
> So what have I got to lose?'

began several of the boys at once. It was the song that had been sung after Katinka Stordal for a couple of years, as soon as there were a sufficient number of boys gathered together and they knew she had been drinking.

'Now that's enough. We shall serve you only on condition you keep quiet.'

Mrs Krane had never spoken so firmly before in her life, unless perhaps to Mr Krane now and again, when she had had to put her foot down. A sudden burning anger came unexpectedly to her aid.

And it did become quiet for a short while. A somewhat surprised quiet. Orange squash, pop and cakes were still being served. But Larsen had got the giggles. Time and again she bubbled over with laughter. 'Oh, my goodness, I know it's tragic, but . . .'

Sønstegård scolded and said, 'Get along with you,' but only as a matter of form. Everyone could hear that quite well.

Mrs Krane stood betrayed by them both. According to what she said later, she did not know any longer whether she was embarrassed and angry, or excited and greedy for more. A curious kind of rage came over her, something dangerous, something she wanted to control, but could not. You can be really afraid of yourself sometimes, Mrs Krane is supposed to have said in relation to this.

The song spurted up again. Each time one more line was added. They were still humming instead of singing the name at the beginning.

> 'Hm-hm, hm-hm's sweet on me,
> So what have I got to lose?
> If only she'd keep off the drink . . .'

'Those who will not behave themselves properly, must go', shouted Mrs Krane, as if in self-defence. 'I'll fetch somebody,' she bawled, thinking of Gjør.

'At this table we're drinking nothing but orange squash.'

'That wasn't what I meant.'

A moment's quiet. Sønstegård was over at the sliding

door, pretending to tidy the shelves. What was going on in the parlour at this moment?

What was happening was that Bowler Hat was saying, 'Don't give a damn about them. What do we care?'

'It's the tune. It's the same tune!'

'Oh, damnation!'

> 'My Katinka's sweet on me,
> So what have I got to lose?
> If only she'd keep off the drink
> But she's always at the booze.'

This time it was like a dam bursting. The boys had come to sing this song, and sing it they would. Only when it was over did Mrs Krane manage to shout, 'We can't have this noise. It won't do, surely you can see that? If we don't have quiet I'll fetch PC Olsen.'

Brave words, which might lead further than she dared imagine. She wasn't one for calling in the police.

It was really quiet for a while. Over by the door Sønstegård could make out a piercing and curious noise, which must have been convulsive sobbing. Shortly after that she heard Gjør say, 'Do they call you Katinka?'

'The whole town calls me Katinka.'

'What a sad state you're in! And you've let this happen to you, without trying to fight back? You!'

Katinka was no longer sobbing. It was difficult to hear what she was saying, for there was sporadic, though quiet, conversation in the café. But her voice had become clear, as it does after sudden, violent weeping, and it reached Sønstegård in fragments: 'I tried to fight back . . . no one who took any notice . . . the only one against them all . . . Some people react only when it's too late . . . when they're already trampled underfoot.'

Then she turned garrulous again as drunkards do, raising her voice and speaking fast.

'If only I'd been able to steel myself when I was small.

If only I'd been able to take a beating without flinching, without screaming, bitten Mother in the leg as I wanted to do, then they would never have brought me to this sad state, as you put it. But I'm unflinching now. Now nobody's going to get me anywhere against my will. I'm well over forty years old, and now I'm going to live as I please and live fast.'

'Now you're going to rise above yourself, Katinka. Now you're going to shake off all this, and be yourself again.'

'Be myself? I am myself now.'

'No, you're not yourself.'

'Rise above myself? Shake myself? How do you see that happening, Justus? I'm a drunkard, I'm telling you.'

'Nonsense, you're not a drunkard. This isn't how people drink. You look for shelter in it and you can get that : a little forgetfulness, a little relaxation. You're hemmed in and don't know where to find refuge. Now, when I've got rid of all these scoundrels—'

'Are you here on a rescue operation, Justus?'

'Call it what you will.'

'You're a man of principle. You've always been a man of principle.'

'Don't talk drivel.'

'Faithfulness, it's called, of course. That sort of principle, I mean. You married again, didn't you, Justus?'

'Good Lord, yes. That has nothing to do with it. Besides, I'm a widower.'

'A widower? Perhaps she died of waiting? Some people do. But what a good thing I didn't leave my children and everything for you that time. It was a good thing, wasn't it?'

'That has nothing to do with it either.'

'No, of course not. What's the point of raking up all that? We might be talking about strangers, after all. I don't care about them, they don't interest me.'

'Now I'm going to throw them out, every man jack of

them. You can give me a helping hand, can't you? Then we'll be getting along, Katinka.'

Yes, there is indeed a lot to be heard before your ears drop off. There sat Katinka Stordal and said that – actually said so herself. And Gjør stood there talking to Bowler Hat as if they were on an equal footing : '*You* can give me a helping hand, can't you?' Of all the things Sønstegård had heard during the past two days, these were not the least incredible.

Bowler Hat's reply was lost on her. The murmur in the café was rising again, dangerously nearing the level of song.

The revolving door spun. A few people turned their heads. In came both the Stordal children. They stood paralysed for an instant, then crossed the room towards the sliding door.

As the singers gradually noticed them the song dwindled to a weak hum or even died away, though one or two kept it up. A few of them shushed the others. A voice said, 'That bighead !'

Larsen and Mrs Krane tried to stop Borghild and Jørgen, without success. They pushed past, simply brushing aside whoever was standing in their way, went into the parlour and closed the door behind them.

Then Mrs Krane found authority. Loudly and with determination she shouted, 'Now you can all go. I want this place cleared.' She also found an argument that immediately put an end to all discussion : 'None of you need pay. All you have to do is go.'

Many *kroners' worth* in orange squash, pop and cigarettes went up in smoke. But Mrs Krane knew for certain that she had seldom acted so correctly, or with such good judgment. She would be able to answer for it to Krane and others until her dying day, a fact that gave her a curious feeling of strength and release. It was to be one of the factors for which she was given credit later on.

Snickering and with some muttering, the boys took their caps, turned up their collars and disappeared in clusters. The revolving door twirled repeatedly.

And this time Mrs Krane had every right to go across to the sliding door and put her ear against it. She heard Borghild: 'What a mess you've got yourself into, Mother.'

'*I've* got myself into? *I* have? Do you think I've made myself so lonely, so shut off from everything, of my own accord? Shut off from being with you? From being human? Have *I* got myself into it?'

'You're not talking sense.'

'Yet you come running after me to get me back on the treadmill again. When was there any point in expecting companionship from you? Not until I walked out on you. What if I had become engaged again? Gone away with another man? I could have done it.'

'Would have been all to the good, I should think,' said Jørgen.

'Good?'

'Of course. So long as – well – all sorts of things. Any old person wouldn't have been—'

'Acceptable?'

'Put it that way if you like. But – but anything would be better than this.'

'Acceptable!' repeated Katinka bitterly. 'Acceptable!'

But Justus Gjør said, 'A kind, handsome, generous uncle, with a motor boat and a car and so on?'

'A boat and a car wouldn't have hurt any.'

'But a poor man, without any such goods and chattels?'

Jørgen did not reply, so far as Mrs Krane could make out.

Katinka said, 'Jesus Christ! . . . Is that how you think?' she added, suddenly severe.

'Why shouldn't we think like that? You grown-ups are so full of old-fashioned nonsense. Perhaps you even thought you were doing us a favour by not marrying again? Of course I don't know whether there was any chance of it, but—'

'Be quiet, Jørgen,' said Borghild.

'I've worked hard, done my best, allowed myself to be spat upon.'

'Couldn't you have relied on us a bit more, Mother?' It was Borghild again. 'Couldn't you have relied on us enough to—'

'Relied on you?'

'Yes, relied on us. You old people take everything so hard. You take everything so terribly hard. We're not like *that* at any rate – so completely— Isn't it a good thing you have us to—' said Borghild, interrupting herself.

'To what?'

'Oh, I don't know, but – to help you a bit. We don't make such a mess of things as you grown-ups do. After all, there is some point in our behaviour.'

'If you couldn't manage any better, Mother, you should never have started it,' said Jørgen.

'Hush, Jørgen,' said Borghild. 'You're just stupid.'

But Katinka said loudly, 'Get out of here! Go away, Jørgen. Get out, both of you! Old woman that I am, I'm telling you to go. I'll work and pray. Try working yourselves, then you'll see.'

'You'd better go,' said Justus Gjør, quietly intervening. 'No use arguing about this now.'

Mrs Krane had only just time to save herself. She almost leapt into the middle of the room, where Larsen and Sønstegård were going from table to table collecting plates and glasses, annoyed because they could scarcely not do so for appearance' sake. The door slid aside, a little stiffly, a little hesitantly. The children came out and walked slowly through the café. They were almost out of the door when Jørgen paused for a moment, turned up his collar, buttoned up his raincoat and took out his best gloves.

'Are you wearing those gloves in this weather?'

'Can't you see I'm not putting them on?'

Then Gjør hurried after them, as if he had forgotten something and wanted to put it right again. 'A cup of tea or something, Jørgen? Something to eat in this filthy weather?'

'Thank you,' said Jørgen, surprised, but far from reluctant.

'Serve young Stordal whatever he likes. You have something too, Borghild. You ate so little just now.'

And Gjør disappeared into the parlour again.

Jørgen had already seated himself at the nearest table; Borghild also, but unwillingly. Larsen, on her way towards them to take their order, heard her say, 'Torsen said she'd make something for us, if only a bit of porridge. Torsen's kind.'

'Porridge? On a Sunday? Two egg-and-anchovy sandwiches, please, and one with smoked sausage. And milk. Aren't you going to have anything?'

'No thanks.'

'Then I can have one with mayonnaise as well.'

'But Jørgen!'

'I'm hungry,' said Jørgen. 'And he's offered it. I don't know what he's doing here, bothering about us, a complete stranger. But it's damned nice of him.'

Larsen went. In her absence Sønstegård made strategic trips around the tables, whisking at them with a cloth and wiping them over. 'You'll manage all right,' she heard Borghild say.

'Easy for you to talk.'

'A boy can go to sea.'

'I don't intend going to sea. But I'm not going to be tied down here by this, either. I'm not taking any worthless little office job and *staying*, if anyone thinks that. Damned nuisance I didn't get my matric first. Only one more year. Father's paid up over and over again. Can't expect him to manage any more.'

'We've had to wait for his money often enough.'

'It always arrives in the end. It's only a question of borrowing.'

'It's not that easy. You are stupid.'

Larsen served them. There was a clatter of crockery, a rustle of paper napkins. Jørgen threw himself at the food, chewing quickly and greedily. Borghild sat looking about her, withdrawn, uneasy, anxious. Nothing was audible for a while.

Larsen and Sønstegård were folding paper napkins again, a task that had become, as it were, a strategic point to which they could withdraw between offensives. Then they heard Jørgen talking fast. He wiped his mouth and helped himself to another sandwich : 'No, the only thing to do is get away. It'll only be the same old story over and over again. She's *ill*, she's worse, she's better.'

' *You've* not been in the habit of taking it seriously.'

'I can still think it's beastly, can't I? All sorts of things make her ill too : if they have a bonfire in the next-door garden; if there's a light, a *pale* light as she calls it, on the eaves across the street *after it gets dark*. As if it can be light when it's *dark*! I'm sick of it all, sick of Father too, and Elise Oyen and all this idiotic claptrap. Old people! The way Mother looks sometimes, that never-ending crossness of hers.'

'She's not cross. Hurry up.'

'What is she then?'

'Desperate.'

'I don't wonder, the way she carries on.'

Jørgen chewed and swallowed, milk and huge bites of food alternately.

'She can't manage the dressmaking any more. If only you'd understand that.'

'If I do understand anything, it's that. But why the dickens can't she? Other people do dressmaking without making half the fuss. Of course there are many good sides to her character – she's marvellous and all that, she meant well.'

He took a final, long gulp.

'People who can't cope always mean well.'

'Have you finished?'

'I've finished. Where shall we be, when—?'

They disappeared into the filthy weather; it hurt to see them go. It was easy to see that they hadn't eaten much since yesterday. Torsen was kind, that was for sure, a thoroughly good person, but where was she to find food? And their father? The way he lived and where he lived – together with Elise Oyen, just about. Each of them is supposed to have a separate room at Mrs Solem's private hotel, but there's a door in between, as everyone knows. And no other rooms available either, since the new teacher came to the junior high school. No, those poor children.

And Katinka? Was she crying again? Not that she had no reason. Loud sobs penetrated all the way to Larsen and Sønstegård, so loud that without hesitation they joined Mrs Krane, who was back at her post by the door. They heard Gjør speaking soothingly. A kind man, you couldn't describe him otherwise. A well-meaning man. A bit too glib, perhaps, when you remembered what he had said about the café just now. A bit superior.

'They'll grow up like him,' said Katinka. 'That's why I'm afraid of their hard-heartedness.'

'They're young,' said Gjør. 'We're all of us hard-hearted when we're young. There, there, there.'

Mrs Krane was suddenly back at the till again. She had become adept at moving her person about quickly. Larsen and Sønstegård removed themselves too.

Someone was coming through the revolving door. As if the whole town had got the message that Mrs Stordal was sitting here today as well – and presumably it had – Mr Buck came into sight. He put down a dripping umbrella and kicked off his galoshes. He made a gesture of greeting, but only barely, a brief nod. He went straight into the parlour, leaving the door open behind him. Plain sailing so far. Mrs Krane took a cautious step out into the room. So did the others.

Katinka was sobbing with her head on her arms. She did not notice Buck and clearly had no idea that he was there. Bowler Hat was sitting in his usual position, his hat on and his legs sprawling. Gjør was standing, patting Katinka on the back.

Buck did not take his hat off either. He placed himself with his hands on his hips under his open raincoat.

'Oh indeed, tears? Well, for once they are not inappropriate. There are plenty of us who might well feel like shedding a tear. Would you be so kind as to inform Mrs Stordal that I'm here, Mr Gjør? As it happens, I know who *you* are. My name's Buck.'

For Mrs Katinka had not so much as raised her head.

'Couldn't we postpone the conversation until a little later?' suggested Gjør. 'Mrs Stordal is on her way home. She can see you there.'

Katinka looked up then.

'I'm not on my way home.'

'No? In that case I did right to come here. As a matter of fact I was looking for Mrs Stordal yesterday too. It's not my fault that the conversation has to take place here. For it must take place. Mrs Stordal has created an intolerable situation for the ladies of the town. I shall be brief, especially as it's a Sunday. I'm a hard-working man and value my day of rest, so I shall content myself with posing a couple of small problems. Then I shall go again. Problems similar to the ones we were given at school about apprentices and labourers. If a . . . decidedly gifted, but negligent dressmaker needs so and so much time for so and so many dresses, how much time do four others – not quite so gifted, but *conscientious* – need for the same number?'

No reply from Katinka.

'Mr Solicitor,' Gjør began. 'As it happens, I know you are a solicitor—'

'No, let me finish. It looks as if my little problem is of no interest. Then let us try another. If an agreement which concerns – let us say hearth and home, a roof over one's head, in brief, existence, not only one's own but that of one's children – if such an agreement is not kept, if no attempt whatever is made to keep it, what will the answer be? What must the answer be?'

Katinka looked up from the handkerchief she was still sobbing into.

'I don't care a damn for your problems. You can't add up.'

Imagine, it had come to this. Mrs Stordal actually said that to Solicitor Buck, one of the most important men in town – at any rate one of the richest. And money makes all the difference, whatever folk may say.

There was complete silence for a while. Then Bowler Hat said, 'You did that very well. That's how to give it them.'

'I still permit myself to believe that I am the one who knows best about that,' said Buck severely, without bothering about the fellow or his remarks. 'I have gone through the problems more than once, I've checked them and so on. The answer will be bankruptcy, eviction, the loss of all possibility of making a living.'

'All right, evict me, evict me. Then I shall be rid of it all.'

'You have two children, Mrs Stordal.'

'Oh yes, yes.'

'And tomorrow is Monday.'

'And then come Tuesday, Wednesday and Thursday.'

'That's how to give it them, that's how to give it them,' exulted Bowler Hat, giving himself a loud slap on the thigh.

'We'll get the better of you, my man. Where do you work? Here on the quay, don't you?'

'None of your business, Mister.'

'None of my business?' Buck found himself imitating

Bowler Hat's accent, from sheer indignation. 'We'll see about that. We'll certainly see about that! There's no shortage of workers these days. In fact, quite the contrary.'

'Go to hell!'

'Thank you very much.'

But a man like Buck couldn't stay there exchanging incivilities with someone like Bowler Hat. He made as if to go, and he didn't look kindly disposed, that's for sure. Mrs Krane shuddered at the thought of having a score to settle with him. Larsen and Sønstegård as well, according to what they assured their listeners afterwards.

And then he showed what a kind fellow he is really. He went up to the table where Katinka was sitting, leant his hands on it, and said, 'Now listen to me, Mrs Stordal. You know I'm a reasonable man, reasonable to the point of absurdity. I make myself ridiculous. And yet I'm offering you one last chance of getting out of this tight spot. For you are in a tight spot. Go home and sit down to your sewing. Finish these dresses you've promised to make. Make a final effort to behave like an honest, sensible person. There are a few days left till the ball, and you *can* sew, according to what everybody says. Then we'll *see*. I shan't promise any more than that, but at any rate we'll see. With a little goodwill on your part we may still find a solution. I'm a patient man, as I said.'

He paused, waiting for an answer. None came. Katinka raised her empty glass to her mouth and put it down again with a clatter.

'Shall we consider the conversation closed for the time being?' said Gjør. 'It won't lead anywhere. Mrs Stordal isn't herself just now. Mrs Stordal's overtired and needs rest more than anything. She—'

'Rest? Yes indeed, when you're on the spree day and night there may well be need of rest. Not herself? When is she herself? I am under the impression that it's been quite a while since she was herself. But if you can make her see reason, Mr Editor, nothing would please me more. If you're able to get her to go home and calm down, so that she has a complete rest and starts working again, you will indeed have done her a service. I personally am prepared, as I said, to go on being patient, to make yet another attempt. The general opinion is that she can work when she wants to, that she is capable of reaching unusually high standards. Ever since yesterday I've—'

'Yes, all those gowns,' exclaimed Bowler Hat.

Buck took no notice. He was not going to stand bandying words with an ill-mannered, interfering outsider, that went without saying. He looked annoyed, but controlled himself.

'I shall hope for the best, then, Mr Editor. But, if I may put it this way, unless work has been resumed tomorrow morning – if not before, I have no prejudice against working on Sunday – my patience is at an end, irrevocably at an end.'

If only Katinka could have kept her mouth shut. But no, she said impudently, 'Mine came to an end a long time ago. You can go to the devil!'

Buck's eyes turned hard, like two glinting pebbles. He was silent for a moment, then he said, 'That's where you'll end up, at any rate. And in style.'

Then he turned and went. Now it seemed as if the police might come at any moment. Mrs Krane wandered about restlessly behind the counter, dazedly righting objects that were standing quite straight, wringing her hands and groaning. Larsen went across and patted her on the arm : 'Don't take it so bad, Mrs Krane. Don't take it so bad.'

Larsen's a kind soul. But, oh God, those eyes of Buck's.

For the time being it was Stordal who entered into the middle of the paralysing silence that had fallen, wet, tousled, and with his usual vague expression. He went into the parlour. They heard him say, 'I suppose this is some kind of revenge?'

'Revenge? Am I to bother my head about revenge too? I've done enough useless things.'

'You always have to be so wonderful, so superior, so much better than the rest of us.'

'I am what I am. At last, for once. And I don't care about any of you. I'm free of you all.'

Suddenly she exclaimed, 'All those terrible evenings in that hideous workroom. Not a sound, not a soul, not a note of music. Bits of thread, scraps, pins everywhere. Ugly dresses hanging there that *had* to be finished. If there happened to be something beautiful, something that was fun to work on, the ugly ones always had to be done first. The cold that came creeping over me – the stoves that went out – everything in the house that ought to have been done – the piles of washing-up – the exhaustion. Exhaustion! The children down here—'

'I believe the woman's out of her mind,' said Stordal, looking round as if calling them all to bear him witness. No one could deny that he had good reason for his exasperation.

'You're right, I'm out of my mind, I'm wicked, spiteful. Oh, how I've prayed to God, or whoever it may be, that it shouldn't eat me away inside. But God doesn't care. I suppose he hasn't the time . . . It all gets too much for him too, I expect,' she added softly, lost in her own thoughts.

Then she was off again : 'But now I'm going to be *free*. Here I sit, free of you all. The more you find fault with me, the freer I become. Loving is a tie. The ties are slipping off me. They're lying on the ground. Here I sit doing as I please. Tenderness – that's a *tie*, stronger than any other. There, they've fallen away! I have no children even, any more.'

'Haven't you? That's an easy way out, I must say.'

'After all, they have you,' said Katinka.

'Very well, they have me. Now I'm told that they have me! And I'm not one to shirk my duty. I've proved it too.

I've paid through the nose again and again. And even if I have to steal, I'll manage.'

'Oh yes, I'm sure you'll manage,' said Katinka quite quietly, in a curious tone of voice.

'And that's the man you were married to? A runt like that?' said Bowler Hat, interrupting the conversation yet again. Stordal gave him a look full of silent contempt.

'Listen to me, Peder,' said Gjør.

'What business is it of *yours*, anyway?' answered Stordal in annoyance. He seemed to have only just noticed Gjør's presence. 'What are you doing here? Is this any concern of yours?'

'I'd like to talk to you, Peder. Let's go outside for a moment.'

'Outside? In this weather?'

'Out into the café then. It looks as if everything has to happen there, as if on a serving tray, so why not?'

They went out into the café. It looked thoroughly respectable, all three ladies in their places and the napkins being folded. The door was open; they could hear from where they sat.

Stordal was still annoyed and his annoyance made him raise his voice.

'You said you were going to leave at once. You had no time for anything. But here you are. And if you're going to get yourself mixed up in this, you can help us to get Katinka home again. Naturally we'll have to see about getting her certified, an irresponsible person like her.

'I am trying to get her to go home. And there's nothing the matter with her, except that she's played out and must have a change. All she can find to do is to play up here. Give her rest and a bit of kindness and she's saner than any of us, with the sanest instincts.'

'I might have expected you to leap to her defence – you two !'

'We two?' said Gjør sharply.

'You two, yes. You always seemed to see something

extraordinary in Katinka. Something extraordinary and misunderstood. And now here you are again, behaving in exactly the same way. Bolstering her up. I wish I could make out why you're hanging around.'

'You talk as if you had complete monopoly of the town. Can't I have ties, too, that bind me to the place?'

'Oh, is that how it is? You left, without hesitation, that poor woman who married you, who believed in you. You went your own way. You had to have a chance to show what you could do. And you simply stayed away. In the meantime matters were arranged. She took it sensibly, very sensibly, got herself a divorce, got on her feet again. Well on her feet too. She found happiness with someone else. I see no reason to keep it a secret, she has every right. Then one fine day you turn up, with "certain ties that bind you to the place". But Elise and I, let me tell you—'

'Who was talking about Elise? The last thing I want to do is come between you and Elise. On the contrary, I'm happy that you and she – well, of course, I tumbled to it pretty quickly. As long as you're happy together it's the best thing that could have happened. No – if I was thinking about anything of that sort, it was about . . . well, you're divorced and we're all old now and it's too late anyway, so I may as well tell you the truth—'

'Katinka?' shouted Stordal loudly, in complete incomprehension.

'Not so loud, Peder. Is that anything to be so surprised about? If Katinka had wanted to come away with me at the time—'

'It did occur to me that you were excessively keen on long walks,' said Stordal slowly. Then he seemed to understand at last. 'And there was I, acting in good faith, the poor naïve husband! Would you believe it! Perhaps it was with you, then—? She came and talked a lot of nonsense, you see, about having been unfaithful to me. I didn't attach much importance to it, as a matter of fact. I took advantage of the opportunity to make a clean sweep, I admit. So it was true, then? And with you?'

'Elise understood well enough. Elise was jealous.'

'I was aware of something. I dimly realized that Katinka had some bee in her bonnet. She's alway had romantic leanings. And as I say, you supported all her obsessions. I didn't attach any importance to any of it. But that *you*—?'

'Is it so strange?'

'Strange? When you had Elise? Yes. But then Katinka considered a future with you would be a bit precarious, did she? A little uncertain?'

'Whatever she may have thought, she didn't think that. She's not like that.'

'Katinka's never been a noble angel of innocence, as you think,' said Stordal irritably.

'And you misjudge Katinka. You've always misjudged her, if I may be allowed to say so. Not least because of that it seemed to me that I had a certain right—'

'Right? Indeed you hadn't. And Elise? What about her?'

'Elise and I – that's another story.'

'Easy to say, darned easy to say. Whenever there's something we can't really defend, it's another story, it's beyond ordinary evaluation. Very convenient, very convenient.'

'Now listen, Peder Stordal . . .'

But Stordal would not listen. He tore himself free of Gjør, who had taken him by the arm in an attempt to placate him, and went on talking loudly and excitedly.

'Then you come here and rush to Katinka's defence, when she's turned the whole town topsy-turvy with her whims. To put it mildly, it must be rather strange for you to find your old flame in this condition.'

'It is, it's more than strange. It's outrageous. You've mistreated her to the point of suicide.'

'Mistreated her? Who's mistreated her, if I may ask?'

'Oh, a good many of you. As far as I can see, just about the whole town.'

'Do you know what you're talking about? Everybody here has done their utmost. She wanted to go to the city to learn *haute couture*. She did so, she was given a sizeable loan. She wanted the children, wanted to support them herself. She was granted that too, practically speaking, that is as far as was justifiable. She wanted to manage as she pleased, in whatever way she pleased. She was allowed to do so, nobody interfered. You really can't blame her lack of success on other people, it's her own damned fault. Some individuals are their own worst enemies, unfortunately. You can do whatever you like for them, it's useless. Katinka, let me tell you, is one of those unfortunate souls who—'

'Yes, yes, that's all very well and good,' interrupted Gjør impatiently.

'But I tell you, I'm prepared to accept the consequences,' continued Stordal, refusing to be held in check, 'which I have done all along, as a matter of fact. From the very first day the whole responsibility has rested on me, when all's said and done.'

'This isn't simply a matter of cash, Peder.'

'I'm aware of that. Aware of it perhaps more than anyone. Here we are, Elise and I. We could have had a home together long ago, if it were not—'

'If it were not for the children, do you mean?' said Gjør sharply. He, too, had stopped wondering whether anyone was listening.

'As far as that goes, I pay for them, though within reason. If I didn't, Jørgen would have been at work long ago – and it would have done him nothing but good. And Borghild would be starting soon too.'

'Within reason? Katinka has *lived* for her children.'

'You can take it from me, she's lived for herself too. For her so-called *ability*, her so-called *talent*. She wanted to be something out of the ordinary, heaven help us. Believe it or not, she's even refused work because it wasn't to her taste, because there was something the matter with the material and the style – even with the customer. Imagine a customer being impossible to sew for! Too fat, or too thin, or God knows what. Your dear Katinka hasn't been afraid of insulting people, heaven knows. But it seems I'm beginning to see more clearly. Oh yes, more and more clearly.'

'You're exaggerating. She may have sent back work when she could make nothing of it. That happens to all of us. But why don't you go now, Peder – you go. I'll get her home, I promise you. And then it'll be a question of making life pleasant for her—'

'What nonsense! Pleasant for her! Try it, and you'll see. Such patience as people have shown her – I'm not only thinking about myself . . . But I'll go. I can't do anything in any case. I know the type only too well.'

Stordal glanced at the clock. 'Hell and damnation, here I am wasting my time. I must get hold of Elise. It's urgent. I ran into Buck, you see. He was *not* kindly disposed.'

'You go, then.'

So Stordal went.

Mrs Krane had been sobbing for a long time. She did not attempt to control herself any more, but gave way to her tears. If only she had a notion why she was crying.

Inside the parlour Bowler Hat and Katinka sat fooling about for all to see. Anybody who cared could listen.

'If only it didn't leak as it does,' said Bowler Hat, 'we could have sat in peace and quiet at my place. But you see what it comes down to when you let people do what they call their best for you. You get nothing for nothing, what else do you expect? The discomfort of giving must vent itself somehow. You must have some rights in return for being kind. The least you can demand is to be allowed to pester the person you've been kind to. You've given them free rein for too long, that's your problem.'

'Thought I ought to for the sake of the children.'

'Yes, those two. They're so unkind.'

'We're all unkind to our mothers to a certain extent, surely?'

'Yes, dammit, I suppose we are.'

'But if you're poor they're after you like fleas. If you're degraded already, the farther you descend. No one can resist humiliating you. Do you know what poverty is? Keeping seven locks on your mouth, among other things. A dressmaker hears women saying every day, "I've nothing to wear". They have plenty to wear. But heaven help the woman who really hasn't, if it's noticeable. She soon learns to keep her mouth shut. If she doesn't she may receive an old dress packed up in a parcel one fine day, or a pot of mutton stew. You saw that for yourself.'

'Hell, yes, I saw all right. Listen, Katinka – that fellow you were sweet on once – he's a good fellow really.'

'Oh, yes.'

'Are you still sweet on him?'

'I'm not sweet on anyone.'

Justus Gjør must have heard the last bit. He had been standing staring in front of him since Stordal left. Now he went into the parlour and stood in front of Katinka, leaning on the table with his hands.

'That's one good thing, Katinka. That you were so independent emotionally. There's a source of strength for you there.'

'Independent? I? What do you mean by that?'

'I mean . . . you've never needed people. In that way you managed without the rest of us.'

Katinka laughed again, that sinister, high-pitched little laugh of hers.

'I managed, did I?'

'I mean . . . you were always dispassionate. It must have helped you.'

'And you thought I *was* like that? Ha, ha, ha, he thought I was. Oh Justus, you are priceless.'

And in the earnest manner of drunkards Katinka Stordal

went on to say the most incredible things to Justus Gjør:
'Take love away from us, and the sun goes down. Take
our children away from us, and our vital organs are
mutilated.'

Even more earnestly, her voice alternately rising and
falling, she said, 'There's only one good remedy for loneliness and revulsion; only one thing that can help you face
life again: *another person's embrace*. Do you hear, Justus,
another person's embrace! If you don't have that, you go
under. You can keep afloat for a while in different ways,
but deep down inside you wither, you wither and perish.
To love, to love, to be loved, that's what it's all about. If
you lack love you might as well lack food or a roof over
your head. It's love that keeps us alive.'

She was half sobbing with emotion at her own words,
like all tipsy people.

'But it's the same with love as with everything else that's
good in this life. It's for people with money,' she sobbed.

'Good Lord, money!'

'Yes, money. You don't understand what you're talking
about. Even you don't understand what you're talking
about.'

'Oh yes, I do understand.'

'Then you shouldn't say "Good Lord".'

'You're quite right. I'm saying stupid things I don't
mean. But am I the only one? Since yesterday I've felt as
if I were taking part in a bad play, a quite idiotic one, in
which nothing is psychologically sound; in which the main
character's talking in direct conflict with her own nature.
Money? Yes, yes of course. But for you to sit there and
say so? . . . Surely that wasn't you speaking, Katinka?
Where did you get it from? When did money ever mean
anything to you, one way or the other?'

'One lives and learns, Justus. Money always means something, one way or the other. But especially the other.
That's the first lesson.'

'Damned right,' chimed in Bowler Hat.

'I must have said a good many wrong-headed things in the past.'

'What of it?'

'I didn't know any better. I thought I was right. But why should you bother about the things I used to say? One never remembers oneself, and the things other people say one remembers incorrectly.'

'One remembers best what was never spoken,' said Gjør bitterly.

'What do you want of me, Justus? Leave me alone. I don't know any longer whether I cared for any of you. Life put me in your way. I care just as much for this man here. I care for him *more*. That's life, don't you see? Nothing to rake up again.'

'I'm not raking anything up again. We never talked about it. I had to leave without so much as a nod, without one word of explanation.'

'Was *I* given any explanation?'

'When you never so much as looked at me? What came between us? Suddenly you wouldn't even meet my eyes. I did what I could to meet yours, to look for a sign, something to go by. After all, you were married to Peder—'

'Had a child by Peder.'

'I thought about *that* often enough.'

'But why did you *say* nothing?' cried Katinka accusingly. 'How could I? A woman with two children? It's a lot, you know, two children.'

'You knew Borghild was on the way?'

'I did and I didn't.'

'Why didn't you *look* at me? Why did you suddenly start looking through me? Why did you avoid me? Of course, even one child is a lot. A lot to give up, if there had been any question of it. And if I know Peder, there would have been. I wanted you to be happy, I wanted whatever was best for you. I waited for a sign from you, as a *mother*.'

Mrs Krane had stopped crying. Tense, breathless, as if

involved in a passionate scene at the movies, she watched. This could scarcely be reality, yet everything else was forgotten. There sat Larsen and Sønstegård; they weren't even pretending to fold napkins any more. And they were real? They were not characters out of a novel? The frontier between dream and daily life was shifting – impossible to tell where it was drawn any more.

Gjør was speaking again. He sounded as though his words had been forced back for so long that they were breaking out against his will.

'That last evening, you were laying the table. I stood in the corner by the door, stood there endlessly. You walked in and out with plates and knives and forks, you didn't say a word. Once you looked at me and smiled. A pathetic smile, Katinka, a smile with no courage in it. There I stood. Finally there was nothing I could do but go. It was up to you to decide.'

'Yes, we have to decide. We have to take the responsibility. And the consequences. And everything else. Later that evening you and Peder sat talking together, and I went out into the garden. I was left there alone. No one came out to me. I had to go in again. I had to suffer that humiliation too.'

'Humiliation? What sort of a word is that? If anyone has need of it, surely it should be me? The day after – my luggage was already in the cab – I ran up the stairs to say good-bye to you. You hadn't even come down. Peder was waiting outside. I tried to meet your eyes again, tried to hold them. You simply looked away.'

'I waited upstairs. I hoped you'd come up. With all my strength I willed you to come up, so that the two of us would be alone, just for that moment. And you came. But you said nothing. "Good-bye", you said. "It's been very pleasant". *Pleasant*! You *went away*. You left me behind in the same old groove. I stretched out my arms after you, I called for you day and night. I got weak and tired calling for you. How I longed for you, Justus. I thought my longing couldn't help but bring you back to me. They sent me to the doctor. Anaemia, it's called.'

'Why in heaven's name did it turn out like that, Katinka?'

'I suppose I was a coward. I was thinking of Jørgen, of – of Peder too. I didn't want Peder to suffer. He was a father just as much as I was a mother.'

'Yes, Peder. You almost seemed to be more tender and more affectionate towards Peder than before. I couldn't make head or tail of it.'

'My dear, we're never more affectionate towards Peder than when we feel sorry for Peder.' And Katinka laughed again. 'Ha, ha, sorry for Peder, that's good! Sorry for Peder. Well, we really are ripping open old wounds, Justus. It's because I'm a bit tipsy. What a long time ago it all was, my dear. Past and gone.

'Good heavens, yes,' she sighed, and must have put her glass to her lips again, for she said, 'Oh – of course, it's empty. Here, Miss, more to drink,' and banged on the table with it.

No one responded and Katinka did not insist. She just sat tapping with her glass, crooning, 'Yes, yes, yes, yes, that's how it is . . . We had a nice time yesterday, didn't we?' she said to Bowler Hat.

'We certainly did.'

Larsen, Mrs Krane and Sønstegård dared not look at each other, dared not steal a glance even. This was a really enormous scandal. And when even Gjør could forget himself, and *he* wasn't drunk or suffering from a hangover!

Larsen crept forward on tiptoe and peeped in. Gjør was standing as if crushed after such a public skirmish. He wiped his forehead and made as if to go. Then he turned back and said brutally, 'Out with it, Katinka. Tell me the truth.'

'The truth?'

'Whether Borghild is—?'

'Don't know.'

'Of course you know. And it's my *right* to know. I – I ought to know and you must tell me.'

'I have the right to answer as I please. That's *my* right.'

'Now listen, Katinka. You were never muddle-headed about things like that. Surely it's not possible that you . . . that you . . . and at the same time—'

'That I what?'

'Oh, you know what I mean.'

'You mean I committed adultery.'

'What nonsense.'

What would you call it, then? Would you say that I blossomed like a rose? That I left your arms and stood in front of the mirror and said, "I look like Eve, newly created"? I remember I did, but everyone thinks that sort of drivel in such a situation, Justus. At least, I imagine so. They do, you know. None of it's as extraordinary as we like to think. I didn't know any longer what was me and what was you – I remember I said that too. You delude yourself so when you're young and foolish.'

'You haven't forgotten those things. You remember them amazingly well.'

'They may well be wrong, all the same. Mistaken.'

'Do you have to drag it all in the mud?'

'I'm not dragging it in the mud. I'm giving things their right . . . their right – isn't the word proportions, Justus?'

'Yes, the word's proportions.'

'Just as I thought, proportions. You see?'

'Oh, you'd better not say any more. And you must act the way you think best. Good-bye for now, Katinka.'

'Good-bye, dear Justus.'

Gjør left. He looked worn out.

At the revolving door he bumped into Elise Oyen, who came rushing in, dripping wet and in a great fury. Gjør took her by the arm with the intention of taking her out with him again.

'Don't come here now, Elise.'

Elise tore herself out of his grasp.

'You're thinking of someone else, as usual. You always used to be thinking about someone else.'

'Did I?'

'As for who it was . . .' Elise shrugged her shoulders. 'I knew about it. It was in the air, as they say. There's no accounting for taste, of course, but really!'

'Come along, Elise.'

'I'll please myself.'

And she continued into the parlour.

Gjør departed, and although he had forgotten himself in the parlour, there was a sense of disintegration and catastrophe in his disappearance from the scene. He had been the only reassuring element here, Mrs Krane realized at that moment. Full of contrition that she, too, had allowed herself to be seduced, in a manner of speaking, by Bowler Hat, she sat waiting for PC Olsen.

Elise planted herself right in front of Katinka Stordal and was no longer good-looking or chic, merely exhausted by snow flurries and anger.

'What did I want with your husband? You might have behaved so that you kept him at home where he belonged.'

Katinka scrutinized her coldly, almost as if she had been expecting this for a long time. She was not in the least surprised. 'He had been on the loose for a long time when you got hold of him,' she said.

'A man like that ought not to be on the loose. And I didn't get hold of him, it was he who got hold of me. Types like that – they hang around you, hang around you for years. And, lo and behold, when you're really fed up one fine day, they stick fast, like leeches. You knew that very well. I suppose it happened to you once upon a time?'

'Do you remember when you telephoned?' said Katinka.

'I wasn't the only one.'

'Morning, noon and night, asking for Mr Stordal. The gay set sat down at the Grand – that was the place to go in those days – doing their best to make me put myself beyond the pale, so that everything could be taken from me. God knows what motives you had *then*? I came very near degradation. I wasn't far from losing grip altogether, from becoming disreputable.'

'As if this isn't losing grip, sitting here—'

'I sit where I wish to sit. That isn't losing grip. But you all tried to poison my mind, to make me petty and contemptible.'

'And I suppose you're not contemptible now either, leading the whole town by the nose? Besides, I thought – I had reason to think—'

'Just go on thinking. You thought correctly.'

'Oh, so I did, did I? If you're not petty and contemptible I don't know who is. Sitting there gloating.'

'I feel nothing any more, neither for nor against.'

'Oh, I detest you! He went and had sunray treatment and massage to make himself look tanned and young. You sat tight, and watched and waited. You could have warned me. You could—'

'You must be mad. Besides, I had my own affairs to look after.'

'Yes, that dressmaking business of yours, that you never worked up into anything. And those youngsters of yours. And what did you get in return for it?'

'Not much, you're right,' said Katinka wearily. 'But . . . young? Wasn't he young? The old affair was over long ago, the new one had begun. If a man's ever young—'

'Now you're enjoying your revenge. But I shan't put up with him any longer,' shouted Elise, forgetting herself completely in her turn. 'He's naïve, he's affected, he has cold hands and cold feet. I feel like taking a bath every time he touches me. I go out into the street and walk and walk—'

'Mrs Stordal,' said Katinka.

'I'm no Mrs Stordal and never will be either. But you never say a word. You sit there thinking that I'm the one who's taken your children from you too. But you don't even say so. You're a sinister person . . . Besides, you needn't think I shan't get my revenge elsewhere,' she added defiantly.

'You'd be stupid if you didn't.'

'Why on earth did you *admit* it?'

'That's my business. I know I should feel sorry for you, Elise. You were lonely in your way, you took a short cut. You must follow it or strike out again.'

'Quiet with this nonsense of yours. I gave you your liberty.'

'Oh . . . it depends on how you look at it.'

'But nobody comes to give me my liberty. I have to do that for myself.'

Katinka shrugged her shoulders.

'I'm not taking those youngsters of yours, at any rate.'

'Those youngsters of mine?'

Katinka seemed to wake up all of a sudden.

'Those youngsters of yours. What a situation! They get nothing to eat, unless I lend the money to pay for it. Soon they won't have a roof over their heads either. You'll be out on the street at any moment. And along comes Peder, wanting us to move in together and take them in. Thank you very much! It's easy to say, easy to arrange in your imagination. There'll have to be an end of going to high school. And of *reading*. Poetry, drama! Now they'll have to pull their weight, both of them, as they should have done long ago. That Borghild – if she can't do anything else she can run errands, I suppose? They're advertising for someone at Berg and Fure's. They come to their father, heaven help us, and he comes to me. As if it were the most natural thing in the world. You've given them a fine up-bringing, teaching them to be upper-class idlers. Borghild going round looking as if she came straight from Oslo, dressed like I don't know what. Filthy brat! She knows how to flaunt herself in front of men already. Talk about the depravity of youth – she's depraved, that one. Huh, and what will become of her? I'll tell you what will become of her, and soon at that. A streetwalker, that's what she'll be. The effect she has on men, and sensuous as she is—'

'Watch your language!'

Katinka had risen to her feet. With some difficulty, but she was on her feet.

Mrs Krane, Larsen and Sønstegård, who were standing together just outside, clutched one another. For Bowler Hat had got up as well. He had been sitting chewing on his cigarette for a long time, just listening, and now he was on his feet too.

'You'd better leave before I throw you out. Tart!'

'Did you say tart?'

'I said tart. I could say worse than that and stand by it. A fellow can see at once what sort you are – you're nothing but a kept woman. Get out!'

He advanced on Elise, who recoiled and then turned and ran. Before she disappeared she shouted, 'Fine state of affairs down here now. A very respectable atmosphere, I must say. Charming customers. Splendid advertisement for business.'

And *she* was out through the revolving door. It whirled after her violently for a long time. Mrs Krane was crying again. Sønstegård sucked her tooth. Larsen was crying too : 'I don't know what *I'm* crying for, but what a terrible afternoon. Simply dreadful,' she sobbed.

'Do hush. If you can't control yourself go out into the kitchen,' said Sønstegård. '*We* mustn't make scenes, at any rate.'

'Quite right, Miss Sønstegård,' hiccuped Mrs Krane.

Inside the parlour Katinka was repeating over and over again, as if in a delirium, 'What did she say? What did she say?'

'Oh, she was talking nonsense.'

'Borghild? As if Borghild—?'

'I guess that Borghild of yours is difficult. But there's

nothing wrong about the girl. The fellows like her. They're after her. Nothing to wonder at. Good-looking girl. That chap at the chemist's – he's a great one for the girls too.'

'But she mustn't . . . she mustn't . . .'

'Oh, she'll keep out of mischief. For the time being. Shy as a hare. Besides, when was it any use talking to youngsters? They're so thick-headed. Did it do any good talking to you when you were young?'

'I don't mean one should talk. I ought to fashion life for her – and for him too – so as to make them strong. I mean . . . if you're happy you grow up free and strong, if you're unhappy, weak and cowed. I wanted – but I was never equal to it. I'm so tired of not being equal to things. That's what makes me so tired.'

'Now listen, as soon as it stops snowing we'll go home to my place. We'll build up a good fire. I know where I can find dry wood. I don't give a damn who it belongs to after all this.'

Mrs Krane looked up from her handkerchief. Larsen and Sønstegård nodded at her : that wretched fellow pinched other folk's firewood into the bargain.

But Mrs Krane was listening to the voice. There it was again. And Katinka said something quite unexpected. 'I must go home,' she said, as calmly and evenly as if that was where she had just come from.

'So that they can ill-treat you all over again. Don't you bother.'

'I must see about finishing all those dresses.'

'Oh, you won't manage it. They expect far too much of you. Listen, if we went away together you could sew all the time. But in moderation. And if I got work too, you could sew as much as you had strength for and as much as you pleased, but no more. I know a dressmaker – or knew her, she's dead now – at home in Sweden. She didn't take on any more than she thought she could finish, and she managed fine. She used to say . . .'

In through the revolving door came Borghild Stordal, still hatless and even wetter than before. Quickly, without looking to right or left, she went into the parlour and closed the door behind her. Closed it properly. There was even a clatter as the rings jammed on the rod, and the thud of the portière against the door. But nobody could move the farthest ring, Mrs Krane knew that. She positioned herself next to it.

'Now we're living off Torsen, Mother,' she heard Borghild say.

'Off Torsen?'

'She's feeding us. She's giving us her own food. She fed us yesterday and today.'

'Off Torsen?' repeated Katinka slowly, as if she had to impress it on herself.

'We'll help you, Mother, if only you'll come home.'

'What can you help me with?'

'Of course – help you – understand you, you see. I expect we've been silly too. Mother, it's your duty to – you're not through with us – surely we can try to help *each other*?'

And Borghild exclaimed, 'I loathe myself. I won't be the sort of girl they go after the minute they set eyes on you. I won't have everything go wrong for me as it has for many of you old people. I'm a hussy too. I don't want to be a hussy. My body wants me to – do you hear, Mother? – but *I* don't want to. I won't get into the sort of mess some of you have. I won't become like one of you.'

'Borghild,' said Katinka. She sounded paralysed. 'Yes, I suppose we have got ourselves into a mess,' she added quietly.

'A terrible mess. It's gone wrong for you, and wrong for Elise, and—'

'It's not so bad for Elise, surely?'

'Oh yes, it is bad, and you know it. Since she was left alone it's been bad. It only looks a little different because she has that good job in the bank. You've . . . coupled with just anybody—'

'Borghild!'

'With anybody who was around, when you . . . couldn't hold out any longer.'

'Borghild! Is that what you think?'

'That's what I must think. That's how it is.'

'Yes, you said a hussy *too*. You think all of us are hussies.'

'I know very well that nobody's as much of a hussy as I am. I'm worse than anyone. Perhaps you were only stupid. But both are just as dangerous. You get *tied*. I see it all around me. And I don't want to get tied. Life's more than just this. It mustn't start like this. Not with someone like him, who's beneath me. I know he's beneath me.'

'Who are you talking about, Borghild?'

'You ought to know. But you sit there in your workroom and notice nothing.'

'It's wrong if I don't sit there, and wrong if I do,' said Katinka bitterly.

'Yes, I'm unreasonable. Because I'm afraid. I'm *young*, Mother. It's not so easy to be young, and have to fight in every direction. You need somewhere to go, at any rate.'

'Borghild! No, it's not easy, I remember that.'

'If somebody like him gets the upper hand – I won't stay here, I won't do as you all do, take just anybody and stay here for life. With children I don't even love.'

'Do my children love me?'

'Must we get sentimental?'

'No, it's not worth it.'

'I want to see the world, but I want to be prepared as well. You still have duties towards us, Mother. You put us into the world, it's your responsibility. And Jørgen—'

'Jørgen, yes. I wanted both of you to get away, Borghild. Well prepared, too, as far as possible. It's just that I wasn't equal to it. You get so tired of not being equal to it. You seem to get blinded by exhaustion. Sometimes even old horses that have always been obedient suddenly kick out.'

Then Borghild said something that really was comical

at such a sad moment. 'Haven't you kicked out enough by now?' she said. But she said it in all seriousness.

'Say you'll come, Mother.'

No reply. Mrs Krane, Larsen and Sønstegård held their breath in suspense.

'Leave me in peace,' came the reply.

'We can't leave you in peace. We're fighting for our lives, don't you see?'

'I suppose that's what I'm doing too, strange though it may seem. I admit it's a bit late . . . Do you know that they sing after me?' asked Katinka all of a sudden, as if she had found a striking argument.

'We know. Jørgen beats them up if he meets any of them on their own.'

'But . . . it must hurt you, doesn't it? I mean—'

'Well, of course it's no fun.'

Silence.

'We understand what it is, Mother, we do understand now. You're . . . rebelling or something. It's because you don't want things to be the same all the time either. I don't suppose anybody can stand it, not even old people. That's why you . . . drink a bit too . . . to get away from everything . . . from that revolting workroom—'

'Do you think it's revolting too?'

'Loathesome, Mother. I'd never be able to stand it. It's only that—'

'Yes.'

'But things can be different, surely? Now we're talking about it at last? In the first place, you can stop making clothes for me. I don't need them. Then you'll take only pretty dresses, the ones you think are most fun to make. When all this is over and done with, I mean. But you'll charge more for them. You can do it perfectly well. You've let them bargain with you, you know. Say you'll come, Mother, please.'

'You know, Borghild' – Katinka was talking slowly, as if she had to pick and choose her words carefully – 'you know, one day you're not up to anything at all. You haven't the courage to do the work you want to do. And you haven't the time to do the things you ought to do. Or the strength perhaps. You know there's only one solution : to get through it, however hopeless it may look. But you get so tired, so tired. And if you can't even pay your debts – you feel whipped.'

'You let us cost you too much, Mother. Those gloves Jørgen got. And now he wants a dinner jacket. He doesn't know any better because he's a boy. There are lots of things boys don't understand. But then you've spoiled him too.'

'I was afraid—'

'Afraid?'

'I – wait a moment, Borghild.'

'Sit down, Mother,' said Borghild. 'Sit down for a while.'

Katinka must have been standing ever since Elise Oyen left.

In the meantime the revolving door had started spinning Someone had walked into it and couldn't get out again. It was Torsen, small, gentle, and totally unfamiliar with the mechanics of modern times. She was really Miss Torsen, but it was a long time since people had called her that.

Torsen was comfortable and straightforward and never confused with Torsen the mason, for he was called by his Christian name as well. She was seldom seen, except at church on Sundays. In the evenings, when she hurried home, there was scarcely anyone in the streets.

Larsen hurried over and helped her out. Torsen remained standing in the middle of the room.

'Is it true that Mrs Stordal's here?'

'She's sitting in there,' Sønstegård informed her. Now, if not earlier, the truth should be told in all its nakedness.

Torsen went across to the sliding door and knocked. As if she was in somebody's house ! Bewildered little Torsen.

She didn't so much as glance at Mrs Krane, who was still standing there listening.

'No,' answered somebody from inside.

'It's me, Marie Torsen.'

Borghild appeared in the doorway : 'What do you want, Torsen?'

'To see your mother. It's *necessary*.'

And Torsen pushed past Borghild to stand in front of Katinka, her hands folded across her stomach.

'You must come home Mrs Stordal, you poor soul. I'll not answer for you no more. It's Sunday, but they're ringing and asking, ringing and asking. I can't get anything done for walking to the telephone all the time. That Mrs Buck wanted her dress back just now, so she could take it to somebody else tomorrow morning, but that was the worst that could have happened, so I said I was doing the flouncing, and it was all but true too. Soon there'll be no one left but young Mrs Berg, but she comes from an uncommonly kind family, there aren't many like the Bjerkems. They came wanting to make a list of the furniture yesterday, and the sewing machine. Bailiff Stigen was so vexed, he hammered on the table with his fist. "I have my orders", says he. They'll come tomorrow and do it by force, I don't doubt. For I said that as long as Mrs Stordal isn't home, you can't make a list of anything. "They'll be fetched", says he, "one of these days". "Come again when Mrs Stordal's home", says I, "you don't get past me as long as I'm answering for her".'

'Thank you, Torsen.'

'Nothing to thank me for. I only do my duty as a human being. But you must come, as I said. Nobody besides yourself can put this to rights.'

Silence. Then Torsen said firmly and quietly, 'I've hired Edwina Dalsbø and Jonetta Gabrielsen. They *can* sew, as long as they're given a helping hand. If we start work tomorrow, all four of us, we'll soon make a clean sweep.

'I'll take it out of my savings, of course,' she added, as if in passing, since Katinka was clearly at a loss for words. 'It'll turn out all right. You *are* the top dressmaker here, after all, nobody can deny that.'

'Thank you, Torsen,' said Katinka again, her voice weak as if she were coming round after fainting.

All might have been well if only that wretched Bowler Hat hadn't been there. He had said nothing for a long time, simply sat chewing on his cigarette, almost forgotten. But he had merely been waiting his opportunity.

'Now listen, don't let them mess you about again. Don't give an inch – give them hell.'

Katinka muttered inaudibly.

'And you believe that? Only a woman could be so green. A mother, of course. It'll be the same thing over and over again, surely you see that? You must keep them on a short rein, all of them, otherwise . . .

'And you can't do that, poor dear,' he said, in that voice, that seducer's voice. Mrs Krane had known for a long time that it was the voice of a seducer, wherever a man like that may have got it from. At this point her contrition reached the depths. For the first time since her confirmation she thought about the word "sin", and about going to church as more than a respectable, suitable thing to do on Sundays. Look at Larsen and Sønstegård, they were hardly patterns of virtue, but the voice had no effect on them. Not even on Borghild, that young girl still at school, who had stood there utterly shameless calling herself a hussy.

At any rate, Mrs Krane said something of the sort later. She is rather overwrought, as has been said already. 'Indeed, I'm no better than Mrs Stordal,' she's supposed to have exclaimed.

But Katinka was maundering on again about her children, just as if Borghild were not there at all. 'Their faces are so childish sometimes,' she said to nobody in particular, 'so bewildered by life. I mustn't forget that. I must remember that their faces can suddenly become quite bewildered.'

'There, what did I tell you? You're caught again.'

'They can say hard things, as young people do. They can kick you aside like an old shoe. But as soon as they really need you, you long to be of use to them. I suppose that's what it means to be a mother.'

'Someone else ought to look after *you*. I'm only telling you – you see, you're like wax, poor dear. The girl comes along and chatters away. She's afraid, for heaven's sake. Needs protection, for heaven's sake. Against herself! Was there anyone who protected you against yourself when you were young and foolish? No, that matter we've had to see to alone, every man jack of us. Perhaps you think you can protect her the day she really does want to throw herself away? That you can hinder it? No-o-o, nobody can, and you know it. You know, too, that you'll be trampled on again, and tossed aside and taken down a peg. Tomorrow, maybe. You yourself don't believe it'll ever be any different. And yet—'

'The ways of a mother's heart are strange,' said Katinka wearily, as if defending herself.

'It certainly seems so.'

'Does it look dreadful at home, Borghild?'

Katinka got to her feet, supporting herself on the table.

'Not too bad, Mother. We've tidied up.'

'Watch it, now,' said Bowler Hat. He was standing as well.

'Are you coming, Mother?' said Borghild, white with tension.

And Torsen added, 'You won't regret it, Mrs Stordal, poor soul. But the other – you'd have regretted that all the days of your life.'

'Oh, there wouldn't have been many of them,' said Katinka, and smiled in apology.

'Poor little thing,' said Bowler Hat.

Then the revolving door spun again. It was Justus Gjør returning, briskly and quite accustomed to revolving doors.

He had Jørgen with him and went resolutely into the parlour.

Perhaps he had heard what was being said. In any case he spoke to Bowler Hat, in a strangely friendly tone: 'Look here, you mustn't pester this lady.'

'I'm not pestering her. She's lonely, like me.' And suddenly Bowler Hat pounded his knuckles on the table so that it jumped into the air. 'If only you weren't here, the lot of you. If only there weren't this gang of people she's afraid of, she'd come to me now. And she'd *stay*. She's afraid of what you all think, that's all there is to it. She's scared of the lot of you. And she's scared of that couple most of all.'

'Of us?' said Borghild and Jørgen together.

'Yes, of you. You have no pity at your age, you see.'

'Oh, is that how it is?' – it was Jørgen.

But Bowler Hat went on with his sermon: 'People shouldn't scare women. They need to be treated gently.'

And he spoke to Katinka again – in that voice, that voice: 'It's true, isn't it, you would have stayed with me, if only—?'

Katinka bent her head without replying.

'You don't even dare admit as much.'

Then she looked up at him with a little smile, gesturing in the air as if slapping away flies.

'You get soft and obedient when you grow old. And I've grown so old, so incredibly old, since – well, I don't quite know when. I was so tired, I didn't know what to do with myself. You were – you were kind to me. I suppose I couldn't take what I had to drink either, as usual. I wasn't myself. And in the meantime I've grown very old . . . And now I'm going home,' she said, evenly and calmly as before.

'Now you're going home Mrs Stordal, poor soul,' said Torsen.

It was Torsen who fetched Katinka's overcoat from the radiator, felt it to see if it was dry, noted with a shake of the head how creased it was, put it on her, settled her hat on her head, took her by the arm and led her out through the café, while they all stood watching with varying degrees of astonishment. Stordal, who had come back again, was there too, clearly dumbfounded.

On the way out Katinka turned once, paused for a moment, and looked at Bowler Hat.

'You know . . . when I didn't have the courage yesterday, there's no other solution. I'd like to say thank you.'

'Thank *you*. But what's going to become of you? You have two friends. This one'll get the sack and will have to beat it, the other's going away too. And then you'll be lonely again with this fine company. You'll have to grit your teeth, and that right and proper.'

'I . . . expect I'll . . . grit my teeth.'

'You must come along now Mrs Stordal, poor soul.'

With a firm grip Torsen escorted Katinka farther. After them came Borghild and Jørgen. Gjor put his hand on Borghild's arm: 'I shan't leave without coming up to see you.'

Borghild gasped and turned white-faced towards him: 'Do you mean that for sure?'

'For sure and certain. You're not afraid of *me*?'

'No, not you.'

'That's good, Borghild.'

Katinka paused again. With an effort, but quite clearly, she said, 'I was thoroughly mixed up, Justus. I was terrible.'

'Now you're going to rest. Have you any sleeping powder?'

'I have nothing.'

'Then I'll get you some. A fellow like that must surely serve some useful purpose and not just go about acting the small-town lion?'

'Who?' said Borghild angrily.

'Nobody, my dear, nobody worth bothering about. A figure, a primitive symbol, but by chance serviceable at this precise moment. Imagine taking a little Lappish idol and using it as a paperweight. That's right, smile again Borghild. It's good to see you smile.'

But Borghild was already on her way out with the others.

The revolving door spun.

For a while nobody uttered a word. Then Stordal said ponderously, 'Well, well – not strong enough for life's conflicts.'

Then Bowler Hat shook his fist in his face : 'You're a life's conflict yourself, you are. You're a clod, a proper runt, that's what you are.'

'Are you going to stand there insulting me, my man? You won't have wasted your breath, let me tell you. You're in the presence of witnesses. We're going to put a stop to all this running in and out and meddling in other people's affairs. I'm going to report you, and then you'll see.'

Stordal ought not to have bothered with the fellow. Presumably it was embarrassment with all the fuss that made him lose his temper. 'What sort of an apparition are you, anyway?' he asked in annoyance.

'What sort of an *apparition* am I? Maybe the one she ought to have had, if Satan hadn't interfered from the very beginning. If only I'd become a fine gentleman like the rest of you, instead of a poor devil without education. We understand one another, she and I.'

'What a lot of poppycock !'

Stordal took the wise course of ignoring the man. 'Well, there's Elise,' he said with relief. 'Thank goodness you've come, my love. It's going to turn out all right, Elise. As I said, it'll turn out all right. But I'm so tired of all this nonsense, my head aches.'

Elise Oyen drew herself away from him.

'Your head ! Yes, your poor head. You ruin everything for us all and believe you've arranged matters splendidly.

That's what you work out in your head.'

'What the devil do you mean? *I've* arranged? *I've* ruined everything? I? I haven't ruined anything for you, at any rate. For you I've smoothed the path to the best of my ability, from the very beginning when you – with rightful passion – from the very right to live, one may say, came to me and stayed—'

Elise cut him off sharply and angrily : 'Rubbish !'

'Rubbish? You call that rubbish? Are you out of your mind? Have *you* lost your senses too?'

'Now then, Peder,' said Justus Gjør. 'Go home now, Peder. It's better than staying *here* talking.'

'You're right. Come on, let's go Elise. Home to my place. We're tired. We're talking rashly.'

'Home with you ever again? Not in this world ! I have my position in the bank. I can be as I was before. I don't need to run away from everything and get drunk with just anybody. I can move over to the Grand, if I want.'

Gjør took Stordal by the arm : 'I'll keep you company for a while. Come along.'

They went, Stordal offering resistance and protests. He managed to say a good deal on the way out, too, directed at Bowler Hat. 'Tell me, at least, what went on out at your place, my good man? What happened?'

'And you think you're going to find out about that? O-oh no. I'm not the sort to throw a woman to the wolves. It's nobody else's business. *What* happened, or *whether* anything happened, or whether nothing happened at all, that we shall keep to ourselves, she and I. Even we have our secrets. Besides, what do you mean by happened? What does somebody like you mean by happened? Only one thing, I suppose. Ruffian.'

Here Gjør managed to get Stordal out, to Mrs Krane's inexpressible relief. All that was lacking now to crown it all was a fight. She was sitting drying her tears again. God knows where they came from. She dripped like a tree after rain.

Between two dabs with her handkerchief she peeped into the parlour. Elise Oyen had disappeared inside. She stood in the middle of the room, biting her lips, then took out her lipstick and improved on them, and bit her lips again. She looked as if she was in pain.

She paid no attention to Bowler Hat, who had thrown himself down on a chair and sat watching her.

In the meantime the evening customers had begun to arrive, the crowd who came to dance. They were normally early on a Sunday. Today, when nobody had really expected them on account of the terrible weather, they were unusually early.

They arrived in small groups, keeping the revolving door spinning. They hung up their raincoats, the men using their pocket combs, the women fluffing out their hair, as people do when intending to dance. They were already helping to move the tables back. In all the commotion no one had given them a thought, and nothing was ready.

As if quite by chance they took little strolls past the door of the parlour and looked in; they had not turned up merely to dance. All they achieved by this was the sight of a very tousled Elise Oyen touching up her ruined make-up. An unusual sight as far as it went. If anyone was usually immaculate in that respect, it was she.

And of course there was Bowler Hat. He was sitting with his legs stretched out in front of him, decidedly something of an attraction after all that had happened. A wonder people had not streamed in long ago.

Over at the radiogram there was rummaging among the records. Somebody put on the everlasting 'Tea for Two'. At once couples began circling like clockwork dolls. Orders were rapped out.

'Coffee please.'

'One orange squash, please.'

169

'Have you any Turkish cigarettes?'

'Three ginger ales, and a plate of cakes.'

Larsen and Sønstegård were already hurrying here and there with trays. To Mrs Krane it was like waking up from a dream. Reality was itself again, as it always had been. Exhausted, she stretched out her hand behind her and pressed the electric bell twice. They would know in the kitchen that they must hurry with the sandwich trays.

Lydersen arrived. He hung up his raincoat carefully, revealing that he was in a blue suit and full rig, intending to stay, intending to dance. He looked round searchingly, caught sight of Elise, who was still standing inside the parlour with her back to him, and went straight in.

Mrs Krane took a trip out on to the floor to watch him. Larsen and Sønstegård paused for a second, trays uplifted. Without bothering about anyone else, Lydersen took Elise by the elbows from behind. Without a word they kissed quickly and passionately several times, went out into the café and began dancing at once.

Larsen, following in their wake with her tray, heard Elise say, 'It wasn't dishwater after all.'

And Lydersen: 'Of course it wasn't – it's plain sailing, then – me again, then.'

Larsen stood as if turned to stone. How was she to interpret this?

She was still standing there when they passed her again. She heard him say, '. . . the future? Don't let's give a damn about that for a while. Been a long time, Elise. It's the two of us after all.'

Larsen hurried away to serve people, was given new orders at other tables, was kept chatting here and there, but overtook Elise and Lydersen just as Elise was saying, '. . . matter's settled as far as I'm concerned . . . but you'll stop chasing that girl . . . needn't waste your time either –

Katinka's going back home. Justus has come – I know Justus.'

'Good Lord, Elise, that was just a bit of nonsense.'

Larsen could not stand there waiting. She was forced to go and fetch her orders, but she wasted no time. Back she came again. Lydersen and Elise were still dancing. It wasn't the proper route for Larsen, but she pretended she couldn't get through anywhere else, followed them and heard : '. . . it used to be Sønstegård, now it's Larsen—'

'What will a fellow not do for credit?' said Lydersen.

'Pooh, I can always lend you that much.'

And then Elise gave Lydersen a quick kiss on the neck just below his ear, like a bite! At which Larsen, who had arrived with her tray, put it down in such a way that everything on it rattled. The people sitting at the table looked at her in astonishment. What was she suddenly so annoyed about? Kind, friendly Miss Larsen?

She herself said later that she saw red when she heard what that fellow Lydersen was really like – Lydersen, who she had thought was so good. For she had, too. Not that she was in love with him. No, she didn't fall as easily as all that. But she had counted him among her friends. And then everything he did turned out to be calculated!

In the doorway of the parlour Bowler Hat appeared. He was standing watching the two of them as well, his eyes following them all around the room, as he chewed on that everlasting cigarette butt of his.

Slowly he lit it and took a couple of puffs. Then he sauntered off, elbowing his way through the dancers, gave the revolving door a shove with his shoulder and was gone.

'Tut, tut, tut,' muttered Mrs Krane, exhausted, relieved and strangely lonely, all at once. She had taken out her knitting and was sitting in her rightful place, behind the counter at the till. She was in working order again, on the surface at least. With her knitting needle she made one of her usual signs to Sønstegård, a kind of conductor's gesture, which she had affected since the alterations. They were getting impatient over at one of the windows. Someone there had tapped his fork against his glass several times already.

'Ginger ale over there in the corner, Miss Larsen. Look sharp about it, please! And remind them in the kitchen about the sandwiches. We must have them now.'

Furtively she dried an occasional tear trying to escape from the corners of her eyes. Why? It was over now, it looked as if it would turn out all right, as they had said. For the best. Perhaps it had never happened? It was almost possible to believe it, as she watched the dancers, listened to the orders being fired to left and right, and kept an eye on Larsen and Sønstegård to see that they were paying attention. The dresses would be finished, the ball take place as it should; people would gradually forget the story, forget that it unfolded here, and come and go as before. Poor Mrs Katinka wouldn't be thrown out on the street, and would probably not behave so foolishly another time. Buck would temper justice with mercy. He was a kind fellow really. Mrs Krane liked to believe that at heart people were kind.

She knew she would cry again when she was alone that evening.

As for Bowler Hat? Disgraceful that Mrs Krane couldn't stop thinking about that wretched fellow. But oh dear, she hoped Stordal wouldn't bother to report him, or Buck. He, too, had talked about something of the sort, about taking Bowler Hat's job away. It wasn't because he would be visible on the quay every now and then, rolling barrels along, or bent under crates he was unloading or taking on board; it was out of pure humanity, because she was sorry for him, sorry for everyone. For everyone.

That voice . . .

No, this would not do. Mrs Krane shook it off. Tomorrow Mr Krane would be home. And he would be angry, as best he could, when he got to hear about all this. There was no need to take it seriously. Talking Krane round was no problem.

Larsen dried her eyes once or twice too, as she cheekily played up to the customers. She had her reasons. Lydersen and Elise were dancing as if in a trance and did not pause once until Elise suddenly stopped, looking pale, with a preoccupied expression, and gripped Lydersen by the arm as if in need of support. He tore his coat off its peg and they left. Neither of them had eaten or drunk and so had nothing to pay for. What a performance!

The last thing Larsen caught was: 'You shall have a brandy as soon as we get to my place.'

To my place! They were going straight down to his place.

Sønstegård saw to it that she stared pointedly at Larsen every time she crossed her path, sucking her tooth audibly, for Larsen was occasionally quite discomposed and absentminded. And Sønstegård knew why.

Once she gave Larsen a little dig: 'Did you remember to get Gjør to pay for what that boy Jørgen ate?'

'I forgot. But surely he'll be coming in—?'

'Heaven knows – a man like that who's on the move. Who knows where *he'll* be tomorrow? Oh no, we must keep our wits about us in *this* job. Not go about dreaming. You rang it up on the till, I suppose, so we won't lose on it?'

Completely crushed, Larsen went over and recorded the amount. She had forgotten to do that too.

Cora Sandel
Alberta and Jacob
Alberta and Freedom
Alberta Alone
Translated by Elizabeth Rokkan
Introductions by Solveig Nellinge

Cora Sandel's brilliant trilogy traces the painful growing to maturity of a woman and an artist. Born in Norway in the late nineteenth century, Alberta craves knowledge and escape from the shabby gentility of her provincial home. The second novel finds her in the Bohemian fringes of Paris, after the death of her parents, facing the conflicts between loyalties to women friends and demanding male lovers, between the prospect of motherhood and her need for autonomy. And in the final novel, *Alberta Alone* she returns eventually to Norway, to write seriously, both to fulfil her creative ambitions and to support herself and her son, Tot.

'As though one of the Brontës had written a realistic day-to-day account of life' *Times Literary Supplement*

'A masterpiece ... it reads magnificently well. On all levels, it is a pleasure to read' *Observer*

Fiction   £2.50

Now in paperback
Janet Frame
To the Is-Land
An Autobiography

Winner of the James Wattie Book of the Year Award, New Zealand, 1983

The first volume of the autobiography of one of the finest novelists writing in English today. *To the Is-Land* is a haunting account of Janet Frame's childhood and adolescence in the New Zealand of the 1920s and 30s. Its simple yet highly crafted language brings alive in vividly remembered detail her materially impoverished but emotionally intense railway family home, her first encounters with love, and death, her first explorations into the worlds of words and poetry.

Autobiography   £4.95

Janet Frame
An Angel At My Table
An Autobiography

An Angel at my Table is the long-awaited second volume of Janet Frame's autobiography. Following the prize-winning *To the Is-Land*, her magical account of her childhood, it records her struggle from childhood into the public world of adults.

While the framework of this book is that of a traditional 'success story', with the painfully shy teenager eventually gaining self-knowledge and self-respect as a writer, the devastating truthfulness of the observations and language make it also a unique work of art.

First British publication

Autobiography   £7.95 hardback